THE DIARY OF PAYTON WREN

Frosted Flames

JULIE PARKER

This is a work of fiction. Names, characters, places, and incidents are products of the author's imagination or are used fictitiously and are not to be construed as real. Any resemblance to actual events, locations, organizations, or persons, living or dead, is entirely coincidental.

World Castle Publishing, LLC
Pensacola, Florida
Copyright © 2024 Julie Parker
Hardback ISBN: 9798322229919
Paperback ISBN: 9798891261921
eBook ISBN: 9798891261938
First Edition World Castle Publishing, LLC, May 14, 2024
http://www.worldcastlepublishing.com
Licensing Notes
Cover: Cover Designs by Karen
Cover-designs-by-karen.com
Editor: Karen Fuller

For my mom, Marilyn,
who said I could achieve anything I set my mind to.
And for my sister, Connie,
who inspired me along the way.

CHAPTER 1

Bear with me while I get my thoughts in order.

Time has slipped away from me, as life, with all its adventures and deviations, sometimes doesn't allow for gentler pastimes, such as looking back. I'm hidden away from the world right now. My seclusion, self-imposed, in a room surrounded by books and windows, even a romantic fireplace. All is quiet, at last. It's in these moments when I sneak away, I find myself here, taking time to look back.

Though I have more modern means of recording a tale, I find myself nostalgic once again and opting to pen this story in an old journal, just like the one Hadrian had been kind enough to give me.

There's something to be said about old, dusty tomes lying in wait for unsuspecting souls. Maybe in an old library, books stacked high upon shelves, all but forgotten in the present world. One day, perhaps, some curious person will run their hands along the spines of forgotten, tangible works. Blow off the dust. Open the crinkly pages. Peer upon the written word almost faded away with age.

But I get ahead of myself.

First, a story must be written before it is shelved, forgotten, and then, hopefully, found again.

So, where was I?

I remember now. I'd left things hanging in the prehistoric world....

I had last seen my dearest Logan six days earlier when he headed out with Hadrian and five other men to confront the evil Alrik. They should have returned days ago.

Hadrian said it took two days to reach Alrik's location. The ruins he was having his followers reconstruct. He'd set himself up as a god, deceiving the innocent, unsuspecting people of this world.

They'd set out with a small arsenal to put an end to Alrik's tyranny. I'd been left behind due to a sprained ankle.

Logan hadn't returned, and I was worried. Since entering the maze, we'd not been parted often, and I missed him. Needed him. His presence fed something in me that was hard to describe. Like he was a part of me, like an arm or a leg. Something I relied upon, which I'm sure I was the same to him. He did not define me. Nor I him. But this bond we shared was unbreakable, constructed by shared experience. Sometimes I felt like a tree that someone shook, removing all the leaves, leaving me bare, exposed. And cold. It's hard when you have gone through so much and can tell only a few. I suppose that's why I take comfort in my journals, and the pen gripped tightly in my hand. Almost like I'm holding a lifeline. Or perhaps an outlet. When there's something inside of you aching to get out. It's caged, right there in your belly. Your ribs acting like a bone-cave, keeping it locked up tight. The jumpiness and gnawing ache of it leaping and clawing, fighting to get out. These words I write are a release. Like a pinprick in a huge balloon, the air slowly, slowly escaping. Give me a moment, and I'll come up with a few more analogies.

Like I was saying, Logan was gone, and I was worried.

The clan was excellent company. They kept me warm and fed and even included me, as much as I was able, in their tasks so I would feel useful. I had to use a long stick to lean on to get around. At night, as I laid in the furs, I'd prop up my foot. Sometimes, in the day, I'd soak it in the cool pond, then feel self-conscious when someone came over to scoop up water for cooking or drinking, and there was my foot, dangling away. Many times, I tried to ask someone if they knew anything about the men who had headed out. Small groups of the remaining men would leave almost daily, just for a few hours, gathering or hunting what they could find, be it meat or another food source. They'd also return with wood for the fires. And each time when I'd asked or mimed inquiries about the others, they'd smile and nod, not understanding. Or of the few words they'd figured out, they'd sometimes reply 'soon,' and I hoped they were correct.

And still, I waited.

Day after day, getting more and more impatient and even worried. Sometimes angry. I wasn't one for sitting on the sidelines docilely while others joined in. And as my foot healed and my temper grew, I began to make plans.

In total, I waited six days.

Then, my foot was healed, and my bag was packed. I'd scoured Hadrian's little cave and found a canvas sack. Within, I'd concealed a cooking pan, a couple of lighters, a backup flint, a blanket, dried meat, and a couple of knives. I'd also packed my journal, filled with stories of the genie and vampire world, and a couple of pens, wanting to keep it close on hand. I also had a leather canteen of water.

To avoid detection and perhaps confrontation, I planned to sneak away in the night as the camp slept. Though I was not a prisoner here, I knew the clan was fond of me. No doubt they would try to prevent me from leaving in what they would believe a foolish, dangerous errand. It was the looks I'd seen some of the women exchange that had made up my mind about leaving. Even if they didn't say they were worried, I suspected as much. It had been too long. We all knew it, even if we didn't say it aloud.

Scrounging around in Hadrian's cave I'd also found some clothing that was more appropriate for the world I was in. Being a bit big on me, the pants I wore had lots of handy pockets and stayed up fine with the belt I found. Hiking boots that he'd outgrown or found too small fit my feet quite well. I remember he'd been kind enough to outfit Logan in similar clothing before they'd headed out. I even had a hat to wear to keep the sun from my face and a few hankies stuffed into my pockets. My shirt was buttoned and plaid. It hung a little long on me, but oh well.

Then I was off.

Nabbing a horse was tricky since they tossed their heads and nickered greetings when I approached. A sturdy gazebo-like structure had been constructed, sheltering the animals, offering shade and protection.

"Shhh," I begged, stroking muzzles and handing out swiped bits of vegetables I'd stashed in my pockets just for this. The mare I settled on was a sweet but feisty animal I knew would be up to the journey. With some coaxing, and more treats, I attached the rope-bridle and a thick mat over her back, which I tied around her belly, and led her away from the others. After we moved through the rocky passageway leading to and from the camp, I climbed onto a boulder and mounted the horse. The sack I'd brought had a long, thick strap that allowed me to carry it over my head and shoulder. I settled it to rest behind me.

Then, with only the direction I'd seen them head off in and the bright moon to light our way, we started off.

CHAPTER 2

Relief surrounded me as no sounds followed in our wake. It appeared we'd escaped undetected. The trackers in the group might come after us in the morning, but if I could put many hours between us and perhaps lose our trail in a creek, then we should be safe.

Though, perhaps that word may be the wrong one to describe this quest, considering the things I knew lurking around this world. Never could I let my guard down, not when dinosaur creatures roamed the lands and ruled the skies.

For now, while warm darkness circled us with welcoming arms and a gentle breeze caressed my skin, I let the bright light of the single moon comfort me. Allow me to pretend, if even for a while, that I was home. At least until a low growl from the brush shook me back to reality.

The sounds I wished to hear, those of familiar

voices or laughter, failed to greet me, hour after hour, as I tired and my legs and behind cramped. What could have happened to Logan and the others? Had they been overwhelmed by Alrik and his followers? Had they met with some other peril? Had they lost their way? And then, I'd curse myself for striking out on my own. Fearing I'd missed them entirely, that we'd passed each other a mile or so apart and never known it. Then, where would I be? Maybe I should return to the camp? I'd second guess myself over and over, and still, the horse plodded on.

As the sun began to crest the horizon, I pulled off the trail I followed. Many times throughout the night, I'd repeated the action, adding to my journey yet also covering my tracks. Hopefully.

The creek, which ran perpendicular to my current direction, was my refuge, and on those detours, I'd urged Indy — the name I'd given my horse — into the water's depth and continued on for a bit. Then, we'd climbed out over the low bank and taken a meandering walk back toward the trail. If I were followed, I knew my pursuers would be cursing me. I wasn't about to make it easy for them.

So, as I crept from the trail once more, this time in search of shelter or a hiding place, I thought upon what my gift in this place could possibly be. It wasn't flight, obviously. My injured ankle could attest to that fact.

It wasn't supersonic hearing, or eyesight, or sense of smell. I wasn't stronger, or faster, or smarter. I couldn't leap as high as the trees or breathe underwater — yes, I tried. I'd also tried to heal a half-dead frog I'd come across by the water's edge. No luck there, either. I'm pretty sure at some point, either Logan or Hadrian must have said 'I wish' in my vicinity, and I hadn't done the genie thing. Nor did I succeed in putting Logan to sleep with my gentle touch the first night we arrived. It had to be something, didn't it?

Indy knickered as I dismounted and led her into a thick clump of trees. Keeping the trail to my left, I'd be able to find my way back as long as I stayed in a straight line. The creek ran along the left side of the trail, and a while back, I'd headed over to let Indy drink and to top up my canteen. If anyone came this far looking for me, they would no doubt search the creek side first, and hopefully, I'd be alerted to their presence. Those precious moments would give me time to escape. This wasn't my first rodeo. I'd been on the run with a horse before.

We settled down next to a tiny clearing with enough room to let Indy graze at the surrounding brush and allow me to spread out my blanket beneath an overhanging rock. It wasn't quite deep enough to cover me entirely, but the sun, which was beginning to peek through the overhead tree leaves, would be off my face. As it was, I tossed and turned, fretful of what had befallen Logan and the others. As it tended to do, my mind went through every bad scenario, making sleep nearly impossible.

Crunching sounds and a low hiss woke me, so I must have drifted off. Indy stomped her feet and tossed her head, alerting me that danger lurked. Slowly, I crept from beneath my shelter, my gaze darting around, searching. Indy now stood frozen, like in a horrified daze. When I moved slowly toward her and grabbed her rope-bridle, I noticed her eyes appeared almost glazed over. Tugging the bridle and giving it a little shake did nothing to gain her attention. Whatever she stared at eluded my detection. I could see nothing out of the ordinary.

"Hey!" I said, hoping to break her from the hold. And then I snapped my fingers before her eyes.

Instantly, a ball of fire formed in the palm of my right hand. And while I was shocked into immobility, Indy suddenly roared to life.

"What the…" I couldn't get it off me. My palm didn't burn, I wasn't hurt, but the flame stuck to me like glue. No amount of shaking would get it off. Careful of Indy's frantic bucks and waving hooves, I moved aside and knelt on the ground. My palm still blazed, and even after rubbing it upon the earth, the flame didn't dislodge.

Something crashed from the brush to the right of me, and charged toward Indy, who reared and screamed in fright. It wasn't overly large, maybe half my size. Black spikey fur and fangs were all I noticed as it flew by, intent on attack.

"No!" I yelled, flinging out my hands in panic.

The ball of fire obeyed this time and rushed in the direction I'd flung it, landing atop the black fur. It caught and held, and as the creature barreled toward Indy, the growing flames instead made it rush off in the direction of the creek. All the while, I could hear it snarling and crying out, mixed with Indy's frantic screams. I was suddenly grateful Logan had shown me how to tie a proper knot so that she didn't pull free and trample away.

"Whoa, whoa." I went carefully toward her, hands raised, my voice calm. She must have noticed my palm no longer flamed, and she settled after a few more words and gentle touches. As she heaved and sighed, I eyed my hand and was relieved to see no burns or scorches. Nothing there to indicate the earlier ball of fire.

Well, that was weird.

I guess I could have left the lighter and flint behind after all.

CHAPTER 3

After Indy was calm and all was quiet, I wandered off aways into the woods to explore this new gift. I couldn't deny that fire was a pretty excellent thing to possess in a prehistoric world. I took a deep breath, held my arm out straight, and snapped my fingers.

Nothing.

Though that was my left hand.

Then, I repeated the action with my right. And lo and behold, I ignited. There was a boulder straight in front of me, and with intention, I pulled back my hand and then pushed it forward. The flame volleyed at the rock, bounced off, landed on the ground, and soon extinguished. In hindsight, I supposed I should have done this at the creek's edge just in case.

"That. Is. Cool."

After I played around a bit more, I returned to my makeshift camp and rifled through my bag. I'd stuffed some dried meat and fruit and veggies in there right before I left. Indy tossed her head when I approached with a couple of hard orange carrot-like things.

"That was scary, eh, girl?" I ruffled her forelock while she munched. "But the nasty hairy beast is no match for flame-girl. Ha. Get it? No *match*?" She didn't get it.

We headed out after I packed up everything, picking up where we'd left off on the faint trail. Before I mounted Indy, I'd looked as far as I could ahead and behind us. There was nothing. No signs of pursuit or of Logan and the others. This was beyond frustrating, but at least I felt a bit better. Slightly braver, considering I now knew I packed firepower.

The hours dragged on. Besides the hum of giant annoying insects and the odd growl, hiss, or snort, I didn't hear anything noteworthy. The rhythmic clop of Indy's hooves made me think of an old song my mom was fond of playing on long car rides—Staying Alive by the Bee Gees. A most fitting tune for this occasion. I hummed the melody but refrained from belting out the lyrics, which I admit I knew quite well.

Before I knew it, the sun was setting. Indy was tired, and so was I. Not to mention, my nether regions were screaming in agony for a break. We went creek side first, and after a good look around, I stripped down and waded to the center of the rushing water. Sinking into the depths, I gave myself a much-needed soaking. Indy was tied off close to the water's edge and was able to drink at leisure. Afterward, the warm weather had me dried off quickly, I was relieved summer was finally fully entrenched. There'd been a few chilly days at the camp, especially during the nights, but luckily, that seemed to have passed.

One thing I was sure of, I did not want to spend a winter in this world. Just the thought of icy cold snow made me shiver. After dressing, I led Indy across the trail to the opposite side and continued in a straight line like before. Since there'd been no sounds of pursuit, I felt it safe enough to light a small fire. Plus, I couldn't stop shivering for some reason. No doubt I'd caught a bit of a chill from the creek. After I tied Indy near some brush, I went about gathering enough stones and tinder to make a little firepit. Turning away from my companion, I ignited a fireball and slowly turned back around. Indy was more interested in the brush than me. Concentrating, I directed the flame into the center of the firepit. It caught on the tinder, and I added some little sticks I'd stashed nearby.

Being chilled made me think about winter again. What if we couldn't get home? What if Logan wanted us to stay here with Hadrian? I tried to convince myself that giant mounds of snow across the land and nothing in the caves to warm us, but tiny fires and furs seemed cozy. Especially if I was with Logan. Then, I quickly pushed the thoughts from my mind when I shivered again.

It wouldn't do at all if I caught a cold here.

No medicine unless they had some herbal remedies. The chances of us finding the medieval world where I could heal would be slim to none. It was just luck that I'd been able to trick that fed into using one of his wishes to get us there last time.

And then I remembered how things had turned out.

How that same fed had died because of me.

I shivered again and wiggled closer to the flames. Looking down at my right hand I tried to will it to warm up just a few degrees so that I could run it over myself like a heating pad. That didn't work. I guess it could only make flames. When I did run my hands up and down my legs, for some reason my left hand seemed cold.

Like, really cold.

When I peered at it in the dying light, I noticed it appeared white. Bone white. *Curious*. I felt it with my right hand, and yep, it was definitely colder. I made a fist a few times, trying to get my blood flowing. Tiny specs of white escaped from my palm. I watched them cascade slowly to the ground near the fire and melt. It took me a second to register what it was I saw, before panic set in.

I surged to my feet. "Is that...snow?"

Indy tossed her head and nickered as though agreeing with my assessment.

My hand was chilly and...snowing, yet it was really no colder than if I'd been outside shoveling for a few minutes without gloves. It wasn't uncomfortable, just as my right hand, when I'd created the fireball, had felt warm but not scorching.

I sat down again and held out both hands in front of me. Was it possible I was both fire and ice?

As before, when I'd been given a gift, I knew there'd be a learning curve. The Payton of this time and place must have been shocked upon discovering her gifts as well. And if she was as primitive as the clan here, just as innocent and kind, I wondered how she was dealing with other worlds. I'd be naïve to think myself worldly in comparison with her, yet I knew the modern world at least, and it would be quite difficult to shock me. She, however, would only know caves, and hunting, and foraging, barely speaking language. How would she stand a chance? Sorrow overtook me until I thought of my own predicament. What I did now and who I searched for—Logan. The thought warmed me. The other Payton would have her Logan at her side. She wouldn't be alone.

My thoughts of Logan seemed to be the key to

calming the steady swirl of snow from my left hand. I noticed my skin was no longer as white as a ghost but was returning to a pinkish hue like my right hand.

Good.

Control. That's what I needed with a power so great as this.

And with that thought, I pulled out my blanket and some food to eat from my pack and settled in for the night.

CHAPTER 4

By morning, the fire had died down, revealing the smoldering embers beneath. Deciding to flex my new-found power, I stared at my left hand and willed it to chill. Snowflakes soon appeared, and as I concentrated harder, a veritable mini-storm swirled from my fist. The flakes fell and sizzled on my campfire, soon extinguishing the lingering heat.

Indy regarded me with a doleful gaze while I packed up my meager supplies and made ready to leave.

"What?" I scrounged around the pack, searching for scraps of veggies for her, but only found a few squished stalks. She wasn't impressed but accepted them anyway.

"We'll find more," I promised, giving her nose a scratch.

The sun slowly made its ascent in the sky, warming the day to an almost uncomfortable level.

Scanning the primitive landscape, I had to wonder if this was what my world was like millions of years ago. Everything was giant-sized. The bugs, the trees, the leaves on some of the trees were as big as umbrellas. Pieces of grass spiked out of the ground like swords. I could take refuge from the elements beneath some of the mushrooms I'd seen. A while back, we'd passed some huge webbed footprints pressed into the mud. The spiderwebs I'd seen made me shiver and I'd avert my gaze to not lay eyes on their creators. I'd seen Jurassic Park. I'd been to museums. I knew what could be out there. I'd experienced first-hand the awesome power these beasts possessed. I had to wonder what our world would be like right now if the dinosaurs hadn't gone extinct. Our population would be nowhere close to seven billion, I would bet.

Indy and I stopped now and then, whenever the need arose, to refill my canteen and get a refreshing drink from the creek. I hadn't much luck scavenging for the vegetables she enjoyed. At least she seemed satisfied eating the green grass and weeds by the water's edge. My own store of food was running low. I'd seen some fish in the creek, but I was so sick of fish that I hadn't attempted to catch any.

Since I'd left camp at midnight and traveled all night and half of the day yesterday, I should be coming close to Alrik's location—if he was to be found along this trail I traveled. Who knew how far off track I might be?

But then, up ahead, I heard sounds. Voices.

Leading Indy off the trail, I moved deeper into the forest. After a short distance, I dismounted and secured her next to some brush. She snorted her disapproval but set to munching as I stealthily moved ahead.

There was a large area off to my left that appeared to be ruins. Undoubtably, the place Hadrian spoke of being Alrik's location. Keeping low, I spied the group of clan members.

So I'd made it then.

But where were the guys? Granted, the area was rather vast, and there were several bodies moving about. A tall person strolled leisurely amongst the ranks wearing a long black flowing cape with a deep hood like the grim reaper. That had to be Alrik. Hadrian said he portrayed himself as a god. Sure enough, as I watched, it was obvious the clan was doing his bidding.

What had he done to set himself up as superior to them? Spark some matches, done a few sleight of hand magic tricks? *There's nothing up my sleeves...*

It wouldn't be hard, I supposed. But if I were to challenge him with my power, I bet it wouldn't take long for him to back down.

Filled with purpose and probably too much

annoyance and self-worth, I broke from the brush and began striding ahead. When I came into view of the ruins and the workers, everyone stopped and stared.

I waved. And smiled. *Lull Alrik into a false sense of —*

A shot sounded, freezing me in place. It hadn't hit me, thank goodness, but ricocheted off a stone beside me. Too close for comfort.

"That's far enough," boomed a voice.

So he had a gun as well. *Great.*

Formidable as my powers were, I didn't think they'd help me against a loaded gun. Or even a well-aimed bow and arrow, as there now seemed to be a bunch of them aimed at me.

That didn't exactly go as planned.

Maybe everyone was on high alert if Hadrian and Logan had previously put in an appearance? Since I was already standing out in the open like a dolt, I had to come up with something.

"Ah, hello? I seem to be lost. Can you help me?" Waved again.

Alrik made a few gestures and spoke some words I didn't understand. Next thing I knew, clansmen were creeping forward, and two large fellows grabbed hold of my arms. They started pulling me forward to their leader, and despite feeling put-out, I refrained from struggling.

As we got before Alrik, the pair holding me shoved me down, making me land on the ground in a heap before him. I turned and faced them, experiencing mild satisfaction when they backed away in what I hoped was fear from my angry glare. I turned that same look on Alrik. Both my hands stirred to action with my heightened emotions. I sunk both palms into the sandy plain, hiding them from sight. Thoughts of Logan and a few deep breaths brought me under control.

"What's your name?" he asked, his voice calculating and curious.

"What's yours?"

"What are you doing here?"

"Talking to you."

He frowned. "Fresh little thing, aren't you?"

"Actually, I'm rather ripe. I've been traveling a few days and…"

"Enough!" He glared at me, and I attempted to smile. "How did you get here? You obviously don't belong."

I shrugged. "I could say the same about you."

He puffed out his chest, and though his cloak hid his feet, I think he rose on his toes to seem larger. "I am a god."

"Really! Which one?"

"The only one."

I got to my feet, my eyes never leaving his. "You

must have some impressive powers if you're a god."

He cracked his head from side to side as though his neck was irritating him. "My powers are not for entertainment. Especially not for the likes of you."

Though I itched to show him what I could do, I worried he'd have me full of arrows with one flick of his hand. Assessing, I pegged his age to be mid-thirties. He was tall and slim but still muscular, judging from the way he filled out the cloak. Broad shouldered, thick legged, but not overly so. His hair appeared black beneath his hood. His nose was shaped like a beak, and his face was tanned from the sun despite the cover the cloak provided. He had on black pants and, high, black boots, and a belt, which was probably where he'd stashed the gun since I didn't see it. His shirt was white, long sleeves rolled up, and crisp collared like Logan had been wearing upon our arrival here. I entertained the thought he'd come from the vamp world.

"I arrived through the mountain," I said, deciding to give him something.

One thick eyebrow rose in interest.

"Alone?"

I nodded. From the frown on his face, I knew he doubted my word.

"Bring her," he said, and with a swirl of his cloak, he turned and strode off.

The two big guys hooked my arms, lifted me,

and we followed after him obediently.

CHAPTER 5

We stopped before a primitive tent made from what appeared to be mammoth tusks, long branches, and animal hides. There were other smaller shelters, but set apart from this larger, grander one. Alrik pulled the flap hanging over the doorway aside and entered within as we approached. One of the guys who held me let go and moved the flap, which had fallen back into place. The other guy pushed me inside. They remained outside. I stumbled over an animal skin rug and almost fell. Once I'd regained my composure, I looked around. The dim, spacious interior allowed for a center firepit, a raised bed, and a chair set before a crudely constructed desk littered with peeled bark used as paper.

Hardly god-like.

Although, upon closer inspection, I noticed several modern-looking gadgets scattered across the desktop. Most I didn't recognize, but there was something that looked like an old cellphone or a communication device, plus a computer keyboard and possibly a laptop. Overhead, narrow openings sliced into the structure would allow smoke from the fire when lit to escape, and fresh air and light in.

Alrik turned the chair at the desk to face me and sat down. "Now, it's just the two of us. Tell me everything."

His tone was much deflated from the one he'd used earlier now that he lacked an audience. I'd left my pack with Indy, but I wore the canteen attached to a shoulder strap. I uncapped the top and took a long swallow.

"You shot at me," I reminded him. That hardly put me in a sharing mood.

He shook his head in denial. "No, not at you. Trust me, if I'd been aiming for you, I wouldn't have missed. I'm an excellent shot."

"That doesn't make me feel better."

"What are you doing here?"

When I continued to regard him with a tight-lipped stare, he sighed.

"Okay, fine. I'm sorry I shot at you. I'm a little on edge lately."

That intrigued me. "Why's that?"

His fingernails suddenly fascinated him. That was fine. I wasn't in a hurry. When he finally looked at me, he rolled his eyes. "I had some visitors a few days ago. It was not a cordial meeting."

"What visitors? From another tribe or something?" I played along, trying to be cool about it, but inside, my belly was suddenly full of knots. I grasped my hands behind my back and thought of Logan again. That gun of Alrik's wasn't merely for show. He'd already proved he had no qualms using it.

"They're of no consequence. Merely an unplanned, unwanted interruption."

"Where are they now?" I tried to sound casual.

"They left."

"Well, they must have done something to make you so on edge," I persisted.

"They seem to have it in their heads that I'm the devil incarnate when all I want is to return home."

"So, they confronted you then?"

He narrowed his gaze. "Why are you so interested? Friends of yours, hmm?"

I snorted. "I haven't been here long enough to make friends. Like you, I'm trying to get home."

"You said you came from the mountain."

"Well, I'm not from here, obviously."

He nodded. "Nor, I'm guessing you realized, am I."

"Did you come through the mountain as well?"

"Yes. A while ago. And before you ask, I have

attempted to return home. Several times. But each time, I grew more lost than the time before. I was lucky to make it back here." He snorted. "*Lucky* may be the wrong word."

The fearful, desperate look on his face made me soften — somewhat. But I forced myself to keep my guard up. Hadrian had warned us that Alrik was a devious, manipulative, power-hungry tyrant.

He pulled back the hood of the cloak and turned in his seat to snatch a bit of cloth from the desk to wipe his brow. His thin black hair hung down around his shoulders, damp from sweat. I could just imagine how uncomfortable it must be for him to stride around in that heavy material all day.

Hadrian had said that Alrik was forcing the clan to build up the ruins here, probably to honor him and his god-like status. But judging by what I'd seen outside, it seemed more to me like he was digging up rather than rebuilding. Looking at Alrick, sweating and frustrated, it appeared he had a different goal in mind.

"Are you looking for something? Is that what you have them doing out there?"

On the corner of the desk rested a basin and a jug of what I assumed was water. He lifted the jug and poured the contents into a crude wooden cup, and drank.

"I'm searching for a well." He ran the back of his hand across his mouth.

That answer stunned me into silence momentarily. "There's a creek near-by." If it was water he was after, that should suit his needs.

"This well isn't to drink from. It has special powers."

His honesty was surprising. Especially since he obviously didn't trust me. Was this his way of hoping I'd reveal information in return? I decided to wait and see what he knew or what he thought he knew. "Why would you think that?"

He took another long swallow from his cup. "I believe the well is a direct link home."

News to me. I knew it had the ability, given specific circumstances, to grant gifts. Other than that, I didn't know what it could do. "There are many worlds. You've seen them, so have I. Why would you think you'd wind up anywhere different going through the well as opposed to the passageway?"

He set his cup down and ran a hand over his face. "It's hard to explain. I can show you."

As he stood up, he pulled the hood back over his head and then gestured to the doorway. We left the shelter and began walking, many pairs of eyes boring into us.

"Don't look at them," he instructed.

I averted my gaze. "Why not?"

"It reinforces superiority over them when they're ignored."

"That's ignorant. They're people, not minions." When I halted my steps, he turned.

"If you ever want to make it home, let them work. Or else join them if you wish."

"Where are you taking me?"

"It's not far," he assured me.

With a shake of my head, I began following him again. Not long after, we came upon a wall of stone. It sat perpendicular to the ground as though someone had deliberately placed it there. Square shaped, I guessed it to be approximately eight feet high and long. Alrik went around the other side. Trailing him, I noticed the slab was about two feet thick. He began pulling away brush that covered much of the stone on this side. Soon, what had been hidden away was revealed — hieroglyphs etched into the surface.

Alrik ran his hands over a series of markings. "Look at this and tell me what you see."

It was a drawing of the well. Whether it was the magic-gift-granting-wishing well or not, I wasn't sure. People were depicted standing around it. Some of them appeared to be inside of it. It showed the well sitting on ground level but also revealed what was going on beneath it — a long tunnel downward through the water, then curving back up into a large cavern. Many tunnels branched off the cavern. As my hands rested on the stone, tracing out the pictures, I felt Alrik come up close beside me.

"Have you seen anything like this in your travels?" his breath was warm against my ear. Shaken, I moved away from him.

It was then I realized we were alone. It took mere seconds to concentrate on heating my right hand, which I'd learned I could do without snapping my fingers. When I turned to face him, I held a fireball.

"Reach for the gun or call out for help, and you'll be charbroiled before your next breath."

He stared at me, frozen in shock. "What are you?"

"Your worst nightmare if you don't tell me where my friends are."

CHAPTER 6

Visibly, Alrik shook. "Don't burn me," he begged.

I almost felt sorry for him. "Tell me where my friends are. I know they were here. It's why you shot at me."

Mesmerized by the flames, his gaze darted back and forth from my hand to my face. "Your friends? Who are your friends? The natives?"

"Don't play dumb. I know Hadrian was here with others."

His gaze focused on mine, his features hardened. "Hadrian is your friend." He spat out the accusation.

"He is. Tell me where they are. Did you do something to them?" If he hurt them, I feared I wouldn't be able to stop myself from frying him. My expression must have shaken him into realizing his life hung in the balance.

"They… left. They confronted me days ago. Threatened me with weapons. Hadrian tried to get the workers to leave with him, but they refused. I give them purpose."

"You treat them like your personal slaves."

"I am a god to them. Everyone needs to believe in something. I don't force them to do anything. They're here willingly. Hadrian stormed off when he couldn't get them to leave with him."

"If you're lying, so help me…"

He put his hands up in the air pleadingly. "I swear I'm not!"

Maybe I had missed them? Had we passed each other like I had feared? It could have happened when I made camp and slept. If Logan retuned to Hadrian's settlement and I wasn't there, I could just imagine his reaction. I'd have to go back. Now.

Unfortunately, Alrik had seen my little parlor trick and may not be too happy about my leaving. He may follow.

Suddenly, the look on his face turned from terror to triumph. He actually smirked at me. "Don't look now, but there's a dozen arrows pointed at your back."

I didn't have to turn around. The sounds of heavy breathing just behind me informed me we were no longer alone, and I no longer held the advantage.

I made a fist, and the fireball disappeared in a puff of smoke—I'd practiced that move, and I could only imagine how cool it looked to someone else.

"Incredible," Alrik said, clearly impressed.

"Um, you asked me about the well. I may have some information," I admitted.

He pulled the gun from his belt and leveled it at me. Then, he gestured at the clansmen to lower their arrows.

"By all means… enlighten me."

***

My hands were tied tightly, palms together, which was uncomfortable. Alrik's reasoning was that if I ignited, I'd burn myself first. I had to admit, it was clever. He'd even had them run a slim rope through my fingers, so I couldn't hope to maneuver them to burn my way out. Maybe if I cooled my left hand, then heated my right? I'd not burn my left, but would I not just extinguish the fire? Most likely so. Plus, it may alert him to the fact I had another power.

At least I was alive, so there was hope of escape. I'd faced worse scenarios than this. Come to think of it, having to escape from terrible fates seemed to be an on-going theme in these other worlds. How I longed for my old, familiar, reliable, boring existence.

"Now, tell me about the well. Tell me everything," Alrik demanded.

We were in his shelter once again, and he sat at his cluttered desk while I was on the dirt floor tied to a pole I leaned against.

"I have to go to the bathroom."

He snorted. "You couldn't have said that before they tied you up?"

"I didn't have to go then."

"Enough of your stalling! If you don't know anything, then you're of no use to me."

"Oh, so you'll just kill me then?" I dared him with my gaze.

He glared at me, and I could almost hear the wheels turning. "I will make you a deal. You tell me about the well, and I'll tell you about your friends."

"You already said they left," I reminded him.

"But I didn't say where they went."

"They no doubt headed back from where they came from."

"But if you came from there, you should have met up with them, don't you think? Now, why's that?"

"I had to sleep sometime. They probably passed me then."

"But they didn't because they didn't go back that way. I saw them leave. They headed North, not South, from where you came from. We found your horse."

I was kind of relieved about that. Poor Indy must have wondered where I'd gone. I shrugged as though it was of no consequence to me. He did have my interest, though.

"Do you know where they went? Besides North?" I asked, wondering how he even knew about cardinal direction. Wasn't that just a my-world thing?

He leaned back in his chair and steepled his fingers, calculating. "You share something with me. I share something with you. That's how it works."

I gave a deep sigh. "Fine. I've seen a well in another world. It had carvings on it. Symbols."

He leaned forward. "What else?"

"It's your turn."

Now he frowned, and his hands turned to fists. "Fine. Hadrian had some fellow with him. He wasn't native."

"Okay."

"Do you know him?"

"Maybe." If he knew Logan meant something to me, he might go after him just to use him against me.

"How did you get that fire power? Were you born with it?"

I wasn't sure how much to reveal. That etching in stone Alrik showed me had intrigued me. And if he knew more than he was letting on, I wondered if it could possibly be the way home for all of us.

"Why do you think the well is a direct link home?" I countered with my own question. "The drawing showed a cavern and tunnels branching off from it. It appears no different than the passageway I came from."

"Symbols on the well," Alrik said. "Maybe that's how it works."

"What do you mean?" From the faraway look on his face, he was clearly trying to make sense of something.

"The picture on the stone tablet, did you notice little strings attached to the people? The strings ran from the tunnels leading to and from the cavern, up the well, and attached to different people. Like each person had their own strand."

"Like a tether? Yes, now that you mention it, I do recall that." Though faint, the lines were there. I'd thought it was depicting water flow or something, but what he said made sense. Although, what was the tether? "Do you think people physically tied themselves off in their world and entered the tunnel or the well?"

"I believe the strands are metaphoric. That the individuals possess something to get them home again. A failsafe. Like a key, or an amulet or something. Maybe it fits into the well somehow?"

"I'd never thought of that," I admitted.

"You didn't bring anything with you when you left your world then? Something to guide you home?"

"No. I've been lost, like you."

He watched my face for a moment. "But you know someone who isn't? Someone who can come and go as they please? Don't you?"

I clamped my lips shut. But I knew he meant Hadrian.

Hadrian who had seemed surprised Logan and I couldn't get home. He'd asked if we'd not been paying attention.

But we had.

And now I wondered if he'd said that to distract us from the fact that he, indeed, could get home.

Whenever he wished.

CHAPTER 7

If Hadrian knew how to get home, why didn't he reveal the secret instead of recruiting us to enter a battle that wasn't ours? A battle I now wondered might be something else entirely. If his sole purpose of taking Logan and the others to confront Alrik had been legit, then where were they? After seeing the clansmen here didn't need or want Hadrian's help, warranted or not, the group should have turned back. But they hadn't. According to Alrik, if he could be believed, they'd continued North. Why?

"I can see by the look on your face you're questioning Hadrian's motives. He didn't tell you his secrets, did he?"

"You know, you remind me of someone." That calculating jerk, Lord Nelson. He'd also been obsessed with the power of the well. So much so that he'd wound up turning his own son into a monster.

Alrik frowned, no doubt reading in my

expression that the person I referred to wasn't a fond memory.

"How did you come by that power you have? Did the well grant it to you?" He jolted me by asking.

Keeping my face neutral, I said, "I honestly have no idea. Born with it, I guess." Which was true, in a way. I didn't know the Payton of this world or how she'd gained her power. Although, past experience told me that she, or someone else, had made a wish. And if they had, I highly doubted the well was buried in prehistoric ruins.

The well! Hadrian was going to the well. I'd bet money on it if I had any.

Maybe he did want to come clean about how he traveled home and back. Maybe he was taking Logan there right now to show him.

But what if each world had its own specific key like Alrik presumed? We'd left our world without one. So, were we doomed to be lost? I had so many questions, but Alrik was in the dark just as much as I was. He couldn't help me. I needed to get free and find Hadrian and Logan.

But first, I had to get Alrik to trust me.

"Do you know about the counterparts? Have you run into yourself yet?"

He snorted. "Of course, I know. It would make perfect sense there are other versions of ourselves in other worlds. Have I run into myself? No."

"You're lucky. I have. It was not pleasant."

"Tell me, do you have this fire power in your world?" The way he watched my face led me to assume he already knew the answer.

"No." If I were truthful to an extent, I just may get him to trust me. "I just discovered I have this ability recently."

The wide-eyed look on his face told me I'd responded correctly. "Amazing. Do you have a power in your own world? And the other worlds, did you have powers there?"

This was the hard part. Would he link the gifts and the presence of the well if I said yes? But if I lied, would he suspect I withheld information and not trust me? I'd have to tread carefully.

"In my world I have a photographic memory, meaning I remember everything I've read. But lots of other people do, too. I wouldn't classify it as a gift. What about you? Do you have a power? Is that how you got the natives to believe you're a god?" I also could recall conversations I'd had as well but I didn't want to reveal too much. Hopefully, my questions would distract him from asking me again about powers I gained in other worlds.

He shook his head and snickered. "I have a lighter and a penlight, a compass, a magnifying glass, and a communication device. The battery is dead now, but when I arrived, it allowed me to use some of the functions."

With how primitive this world was, it wouldn't take much to make the clan think someone was a god. A Swiss army knife would probably suffice.

"How many moons in your world?" I had to ask.

"You mean that large glowing orb in the sky that seems to cause quite a ruckus with the natives?"

"You don't know what a moon is?"

"If that's what you call it, there isn't one of those in my world. Although, I have noticed some worlds have one, or more than one."

"My world has one. Same as here," I said.

"Perhaps this is the same world as yours, but another time."

I shrugged. So, he knew about the time anomaly as well. "Why would you remain here? If I hadn't met up with Hadrian, I would have left soon after arriving. There are actual dinosaurs here."

"It's not so bad." His gaze seemed far away suddenly. "The fires seem to keep the monsters at bay. I've seen worse places. Much worse."

I had to wonder how much of his decision was weighted by the fact he enjoyed god-like status here. "How long have you been gone?"

Now, his expression became almost haunted. "It's been over a year. You?"

"A couple of months. You and Hadrian are the first I've come across who were also travelers. Besides the other me, that is."

"Hadrian," he spat. "He's no fellow traveler. He comes and goes as he pleases."

"He was surprised I couldn't get home," I admitted. "He asked if I'd not been paying attention." The strife between Alrik and Hadrian was curious. Being fellow travelers, you'd think they would be bonded over their experience. But, as Alrik pointed out, our circumstances were not similar. Hadrian wasn't lost like we were.

"He's a liar. There is a way home, but he will not share it with me. Nor you, I think."

"Why, though? What's it to him if we get home? Is he afraid of being alone here? I mean, he seems to have made a good life for himself. Maybe his world isn't so great?"

"Who knows his reasoning? He doesn't share anything with me. When I first arrived, he was here. I know about the cave settlement where he and his native friends live. They allowed me to stay with them... in the beginning. But then Hadrian asked me to leave. Said I asked too many questions. That I intimidated the clan. I'd shown them my tricks and it wasn't my fault they began to worship me. When I left, I wasn't alone. Many of Hadrian's so-called friends left with me, and several others joined us afterward. That's why he hates me. When we arrived here at these ruins, I became aware of the drawings on the stone tablet. None of the natives here knew the exact location of the well. I assumed it made sense that it was nearby."

I contemplated him a moment. "I have to go back. I can't learn anything being here."

Alrik's expression was difficult to read. At last, he sighed. "You're right. If you return to him, maybe you can learn his secrets. I only hope if you discover the way to get home, you won't forget about me."

"I won't," I promised.

Then he reached down into his boot and pulled out a long dagger.

I gulped. "Are you going to cut me free?"

"Do you take me for a fool? I'm going to kill you."

Then he laughed. Hard.

"You… should see… the look… on your face."

He cut the ropes to my hands.

I didn't find his humor remotely amusing. Although, to be fair, after the fireball incident, I guess he owed me a scare.

CHAPTER 8

Alrik invited me to spend the night in camp, but I declined his offer. Something about him made me uneasy, and though we'd forged a tenuous truce, I couldn't bring myself to trust him. They'd returned Indy to me, and my pack, in which they'd kindly added some supplies to see me home. Indy nickered when she saw me. I scratched her nose and ruffled her mane. Alrik stood by as I mounted and prepared to leave. The area was well lit by numerous small fires, and I remembered what he'd said about fire keeping the beasts at bay. As tempted as I was to aim Indy North and seek out Logan and Hadrian, I had no idea where they were headed, and I couldn't risk missing them.

"Good luck to you," Alrik said.

"And you."

I headed off, picking up the trail leading back to Hadrian's caves, the light of a torch warding off the darkness. Though it was late, I wasn't tired, and I knew I could last a few hours before bedding down somewhere for the night. This time, I would stay creek-side.

Hours later, after pondering all I'd learned in my short time with Alrik and admiring my flawless escape, I pulled off the trail. I set up camp, had a bit to eat, then spread out my blanket and laid next to the fire I'd made. Indy, tied nearby, was content to munch on the long grass beside the creek. My thoughts turned to Logan as they generally did when I settled down alone. What was he doing right now? Was he thinking of me? No doubt he thought me safe back at camp, so he wouldn't be as worried as I was about him. And then I wondered about the mysterious Hadrian. Was he revealing the secrets of the well to Logan? Or was he holding tight to his information, fearing the truth may be the end of our presence here? I rolled over and drifted off, only to wake later to Indy's loud whinny.

Leaping to my feet, I held both hands out, ready for battle. One, already aflame, the other, becoming cold as ice. My little fire had died down, but it was still night as darkness yet surrounded the land.

"What's wrong?" I hissed at Indy, who tossed her head and fought the rope that held her. My frantic gaze was everywhere.

In the nearby woods, the light of many torches

appeared and began surrounding us. Though I tried to calm myself, to call back the fear that made my hands react, my racing heart worked against me. How could I help Indy settle when I couldn't control my own emotions that were abounding with panic?

"Who's there?" I demanded. "Come out, make yourself known." Had Alrik changed his mind and sent his followers after me?

"Payton?" I heard my name on familiar lips.

"Logan?" Was it truly him?

He burst into the clearing, and when he would have rushed to take me into his arms, I cried out, "No!"

Seeing the fire in my palm, he quickly realized my dilemma. And as I sought to cover my indisposition from the others who began emerging from the brush, I made a dive for the creek and thrust my hands into the watery depths.

"Help me with the horse," Logan called out and gestured at Indy, attempting to gain attention, shielding me from curious eyes.

"Payton? Is that you?" I heard Hadrian call out.

"It's me," I admitted, willing my heart and hands to calm. Finally, I sensed my temperature return to normal. I rose from the side of the creek and faced the group who'd left several days ago.

Hadrian came toward me. "Payton, what are you doing out here? Are you traveling alone?" His tone was curious and slightly chastising, which I didn't appreciate.

"No. I brought a horse," I said, then felt stupid because I knew that wasn't what he meant.

Logan, at last having calmed Indy, secured her rope and came over to stand beside Hadrian. My gaze feasted on him, quickly scanning for any signs of injury. When he reached out his arms this time, I didn't hesitate to rush into them. I felt his lips on my hair, the familiar scent of him surrounding me.

Reluctantly, I allowed him to pull away so he could inspect me as well. "You're all right?" he asked.

I nodded. "You?"

"Fine."

"What are you doing out here?" he repeated Hadrian's question.

"I... you guys were gone a long time. You said it would take two days to get to Alrik. You were gone six days before I left. I was worried."

The guys exchanged a glance. I watched them with a frown, not liking this alliance between them that left me out. Now that the excitement was over, I noticed the torch light moving around in the forest as the clansmen retrieved their horses and brought them to the river to drink.

"Might as well make camp here since you've already got a bit of a fire going," Hadrian said. He stared at me a moment longer, his expression hard to read in the dim light, and then he gave a nod and moved off to tend to his horse.

Logan led me over to sit by the fire. He added some sticks that I'd laid out beside the circle of rocks, urging the dwindling flames back to life.

"Logan... I..."

He shook his head once. "We'll talk about it later." He looked pointedly at my hands.

"Where were you?"

"We'll talk about that later too."

Frustrating. I came here searching for answers, and all I found were more questions.

Hadrian soon joined us, taking a seat across the firepit from where Logan and I sat shoulder to shoulder, his hand gripped in mine.

"I think somebody missed you." Hadrian gave Logan a wink.

"I did miss him," I admitted. "I was worried. You guys were gone so long."

Hadrian had a long stick in his hand that he used to poke at the fire. "Sorry. Didn't mean to worry you. We had some trouble on the second day out, which made us have to take it slow."

"Nothing serious, I hope?"

"No," Hadrian replied. "One of the horses was spooked and twisted its leg. We had to take a lot of breaks and apply cold compresses, so it doubled our time getting to Alrik's camp. Then, we didn't head right back afterward."

"Obviously," I said.

"I'm glad we found you now," Logan rushed to say, cutting off what he knew would be me venting my annoyance. "Just a little further up, and you'd be at the ruins with Alrik."

My gut warned me not to admit in front of Hadrian that it was exactly where I'd come from. If he had secrets, so would I. At least Indy seemed pleased to be reacquainted with her horse buddies mingling around her. She tossed her head and stomped her foot as though telling a great tale.

"It's late," Logan said. He got up, retrieved his bedroll, and laid it out beside my blanket.

Hadrian, taking the hint, got his as well and put it down across the fire from us. The rest of the men had set up their bedrolls and another fire a short way downstream, allowing us our privacy to talk, I supposed.

"We'll head back in the morning. We can talk then," Hadrian said, laying down, his head resting on his hands.

Logan and I curled up together. Using his arm as a pillow, I soon fell asleep.

CHAPTER 9

We returned to the caves the next morning. Logan and I rode side by side, and Hadrian rode in front, leading the group. We were all close enough to carry on conversation easily, so Logan and I refrained from discussing anything confidential. I knew he was anxious to talk to me about stuff. First, in his mind, no doubt was my new power. And he only knew the half of it. The way he watched Hadrian's back made me wonder what he'd discovered and how it would bode for us.

As much as I wanted to confront Hadrian with what Alrik had told me, I knew I'd first have to come clean about making it to the ruins. That conversation needed to be face to face, so I could watch Hadrian's expression closely. The way he'd stared at me last night made me wonder if he was nervous that I had spoken with Alrik and maybe learned things that Hadrian would rather be kept secret.

The purpose of the group coming out here had been to confront Alrik and his exploitation of the clan. I wondered if there'd been any chance for discussion between the parties? If so, Logan may be aware already of Alrik's suspicions and theories about Hadrian? Perhaps that had spurred the abrupt detour North? I'd have to wait and see if they'd gone to the well or somewhere else.

We pulled off toward the creek to stretch our legs and water the horses after several hours of riding. At the water's edge, I dangled my bare feet in the cool current. Logan joined me, sitting close, and passed me a bit of dried meat to chew on.

"Yuck. My teeth are protesting," I complained but refrained from returning his offering.

His own teeth were chomping enthusiastically. "It's kinda like jerky. But a lot tougher."

"Something else to make me long for home." I let loose a sigh.

"Come on, it's not so bad," Hadrian said, coming to stand over us.

He seemed to want to keep us close or keep us from discussing anything without him being there. Or maybe I was just being paranoid? He must have been speculating if something was up, considering the tension in the air.

"I had to borrow a few things from your cave,"

I admitted. "I hope you don't mind."

He shrugged. "Not at all. I'm sorry you felt the need to come after us. I hope your ankle is healed up."

I wiggled my foot around. "Yeah, it's good now. And it's okay. Logan could tell you I'm not the most patient person. I'm not one for sitting around."

Logan chuckled. "No, really? Never would have guessed."

Hadrian was smiling when I looked up at him over my shoulder.

"I knew you wanted to go with us. Shame that you got hurt."

Now, I shrugged. "Oh well. We're all together now, safe and sound. That's all that matters." He gave me that look again, like he was trying to see inside me. Then his smile returned, and I questioned whether I was reading more into it than I should. Maybe Alrik was full of it and had just planted seeds of doubt to make me question our new friendship?

"Ready to get going?" Logan aimed that question at Hadrian.

"Yeah. I have a feeling Payton wasn't the only one back at the caves wondering where we got to," Hadrian answered.

"I did notice a lot of hand-wringing and worried looks," I said.

"Comes with the territory," Hadrian remarked

as he began readying his horse. "As you saw when you first arrived, there's a lot of dangerous things roaming around."

"You got that right," Logan readily agreed. He got to his feet and reached out his hand to me, but I waved him off. I shook my wet feet before pulling on my footwear.

"You didn't run into anything, did you?" Logan asked me.

"Um. Kinda. But it got scared by something and took off," I eluded. He must have noticed my warning expression since he didn't ask me to elaborate.

"We had a couple of close calls as well," Hadrian said. "Just some wild boars and such. Nothing we couldn't handle."

"That's good." I didn't care for the idea of Logan being out here vulnerable. Of course, I had been as well until I discovered my gift. But really, despite what I now knew I could do, it had been foolhardy to head out alone.

"I think being in a group like this helps. Plus, at night, we always had fire, which keeps most things away," Hadrian said.

I almost said, 'Yeah, that's what Alrik said too,' then nearly bit my tongue off, stopping the words from leaving my mouth.

"I'm sure it'll be clear sailing from here to home,"

Logan said cheerfully, no doubt trying to overcome the tension still floating around.

So, of course, as if on cue, that's when all hell broke loose.

The horses, possessing an uncanny sixth sense for danger, began screaming and rearing. Some of them hadn't been properly secured or had been in the process of being untied and getting ready to leave. The ones who got free bolted. The others continued to freak out.

Logan and I moved back to back, assuming a readiness stance. Hadrian held tight to the reins of his horse, attempting to calm him.

"What is it?" I tried to spot where the danger was but saw nothing.

Then I looked up.

"Logan! Up there." Atop the trees was a huge bird perched precariously on a branch that looked about ready to snap. Its talons were massive, probably twice the size of Logan's hands. Its beak was over a foot long, the top curved down at the end like a hook. Beady black eyes watched our every move. If I wasn't so afraid, I might have admired its beautiful dark feathers, the glinting sun-catching hues of blue and purple.

Most of the clansmen had scattered, tearing after their mounts. Even now I could hear crashing through the brush and screams, both human and animal. As I watched the bird creature, something else angled across the sky.

"There's more of them," I warned.

"Damn it!" Hadrian, holding his horse's reins in one hand, reached behind him with his free hand and pulled a gun from his belt. Taking careful aim, he fired a shot at the bird perched in the tree. The shot deflected off its beak, making its head snap to the left. Not waiting to see what happened next, he leapt onto his horse's back and charged away in the direction of the chaos, leaving Logan and me to fend for ourselves. Both of us now trained our eyes on the bird. When it turned back, glaring defiantly, it spread its massive wings and squawked. The branch broke suddenly, and thrown off balance, the bird jolted to the right, then glided to the ground with a thump. It took menacing steps toward us.

"Stay back!" I moved swiftly in front of Logan.

When he would have pushed me behind him, I raised my flaming palm and told him, "No!".

The bird's eyes narrowed, seeing the fire I held. It squawked its rage and rose up tall on its talons, wings spread wide. Flapping, it attempted to blow out the flames, as crazy as that seemed.

"I don't know about you," I hollered. "But I'm in the mood for roasted chicken."

"So am I," Logan hollered back. He'd moved further behind me and off to the side. I gauged his whereabouts by the way the bird's head swiveled back and forth between us.

"Back off, buzzard! I'm warning you." I flung a fireball at its feet, then quickly made another and flung that one as well. Retreating a few steps, it seemed to ponder its next move. I realized how calculating and intelligent the creature was.

Chilling my left hand, I made a snowball and lobbed it to Logan.

"Holy shit, you can make fire *and* ice!" I took a second to bask in his impressed tone.

"Throw it," I instructed. He was a better shot than me.

Soon, we were blasting the bird with snow and fire balls until it finally shook its head and flew off, squawking its fury.

Seeing the imminent danger had passed, Logan waited while I gained control over my hands.

"The horses," I reminded him. And quickly, he saw to them. It took us only a minute or so to calm them enough before we leapt on their backs and charged off to find Hadrian and the others.

CHAPTER 10

The return to the caves was a solemn affair. Two of the clansmen had perished in the attack, and a horse had been found dead. Another horse had charged off, and we were unable to catch it.

Hadrian was desolate over the loss of his friends, blaming himself despite the unforeseen attack. There'd been nothing else to do but collect what we could and start back on the trail again. I overheard Logan telling him that the bird he'd shot flew off, so I knew he wasn't ready to share news of my powers with him yet.

We rode on, and with only short rests, we continued at night by torchlight, all of us anxious to reach the safety of the caves. Making good time, we arrived exhausted in the late afternoon of the next day.

Many crowded around to greet us, and it wasn't long before the wails of the families who'd lost loved ones began. My heart broke for these gentle people who endured life in an unforgiving and unpredictable world.

Tired to the bone, Logan and I ate a light meal and retired to our cave. Though not yet evening, he sparked up the fire by the entranceway, and we settled down in the furs together. My head resting on his shoulder, I felt his breath turn deep and steady as sleep settled over him. Despite my own exhaustion, sleep eluded me. Soon there would be a conversation with Hadrian, and I wasn't looking forward to it.

Maybe he did have a way to get home. But our hopes would be dashed if there was, in fact, a key, possibly only obtained from his original world, allowing him to do so. What if that was the case? Would we be doomed to roam the tunnels for years just as old Logan and Payton had done?

It could be the reason Hadrian had refrained from telling us the truth.

He most likely realized that since we admitted to being lost, we hadn't brought a key from our world to return home. And telling us so would only cement the reality of our situation.

But what if Alrik was right, and there was a way to reach home, and Hadrian was keeping it from us? How would we know the truth? He could easily lie if he'd decided he wanted us to remain. Part of me wished Logan would wake up so we could finally talk in private.

Hearing him snort, I gave up the idea and tried again to sleep.

There would be plenty of time to talk once we rested.

***

Hours later, while night still bathed the land in darkness, Logan bolted upright, a gasp escaping him.

"Are you okay?" Still groggy from sleep, I reached out to him.

He was covered in cool sweat.

"Yeah. Bad dream." He ran a hand over his face, then looked at the entrance to the cave. "It's probably almost morning. We should talk before everyone wakes up."

"Good idea."

Moving the furs aside, I reached for a canteen and passed it to him. He swallowed a few times, then passed it back to me. I drank as well.

"Do you want to start, or should I?"

"I will." Setting aside the canteen, I pulled the fur around me and got comfortable. "You know I can make fire and ice…which I discovered… before I talked with Alrik." I made sure to keep my voice low in case anyone—like Hadrian—was lurking around close by.

"I knew it! I had a feeling you'd seen him. Man, do you know how foolish that was going there—"

"I know," I interrupted. "But, like I said, I wasn't

helpless."

"Maybe so, but you need to be pretty close to your target to use your powers. Not the best defense against bows and arrows or a gun..." He paused and took in my shifty-eyed gaze. "Which you realized after you confronted him, right?"

"Um, yes."

I could almost see the steam come out of his ears.

"Before you get all weird, I have important things to tell you. I had a conversation with Alrik, and I found out some stuff. Stuff about Hadrian."

His eyebrow arched. "What kind of stuff."

"I have a feeling you learned a few things too. Anyway, Alrik told me he met Hadrian when he first arrived in this world. Hadrian took him in and let him live here at the caves until Alrik got a little too friendly with the clan. He'd been showing off his gadgets, and they believed he had godly powers. So Hadrian ousted him. Alrik left, but he wasn't alone. Some of the clansmen chose to leave with him, and some followed later."

"Wow."

"Alrik believes Hadrian can get home. That he has some sort of key or something which works hand in hand with the well. Yes, he knows about the well. And there's also hieroglyphs of it too, but anyway, can you imagine? That's what Alrik is doing at the ruins — looking for the well. He's trying to get home."

"Okay."

"Okay? That's it?"

He let loose a big sigh. "Hadrian admitted to me that he can get home."

"Okay, well, we both knew that when we talked to him before. Remember, he was surprised when we said we couldn't, and he said something about us not paying attention. So, how does he do it? Is he just really lucky, or does he use a key? And if so, did he get it from his world? Did we have one in our world that we stupidly left behind, and now we're trapped here forever just like old Logan—"

"Wait." It was his turn to interrupt me. "There isn't a key. At least, not as far as I know."

My jaw clicked as my mouth opened and closed a few times while I processed. "Then how?"

"First, I have to tell you that things weren't as we thought they were. The doors... they don't stay in one place."

"What? What does that mean?"

He looked annoyed, but not with me. "It means that the map you kept drawing was useless. The tunnels stay the same, but the worlds beyond the doors keep shifting, changing, rotating, and spinning, like the earth."

The reality of what he said landed hard in my stomach like a stone. "Then that means we'll never figure out the way home."

But then what else he'd said sunk in.

"So how does Hadrian do it?"

Logan looked down, not meeting my gaze. "I don't know. He hasn't said."

Now I was annoyed. "Just like what Alrik said to me. Hadrian has secrets he's not willing to share. If he won't tell us, then he's keeping us here against our will."

"I know you're upset, but it could be that it only works for him and his world. It may not work for us. We'll figure it out. I promise. I want to hear more about what happened with Alrik. What else did he say? And what do you mean there's hieroglyphs?"

What Logan said made sense, it was what I'd pondered as well. Maybe Hadrian was just sparing us more heartache? We wouldn't know until we talked with him at length about it.

CHAPTER 11

"There's a large stone tablet with ancient drawings of a well," I began.

"What is it with that well? There must be one in every world causing chaos," Logan spat.

From the tone of his voice, I could tell how exasperated and exhausted he was. This was taking a toll on us both. All the unknowns. All the risks. All the dashed hopes, along with missing home and our families so much, it'd become an almost physical ache.

"So, when I first arrived there, Alrik was immediately suspicious. He was on edge because you guys had recently confronted him. It took a bit of talking, but I finally convinced him I was a fellow traveler and just looking for answers." The frown creases on Logan's face got deeper, and I knew he was biting his tongue. For that reason, I decided to leave out some bits about what had transpired.

"He wound up showing me the stone tablet

with the drawing of the well. The cool thing was it also depicted people around the well and — get this — *in* the well." Before he could interrupt me, I rushed on. "There were these lines on the people that swirled into the well. At first, I thought it was showing a water current or something. But Alrik said the lines were tethers. That each person was metaphorically tethered to their world so that they could return. People were entering the well. Swimming down deep and coming up in a cavern which had a bunch of tunnels branching off it. Just like the tunnels we came from."

"Holy shit."

"Right?" I was glad he thought this was as important as I did. "Alrik thinks the well is the way home. He doesn't have the natives building him a temple in those ruins to worship him as a god. He's got them digging around looking for the well."

"He thinks he can get home through the well as opposed to the other tunnels?"

"Maybe. He's not sure. But he seems to believe Hadrian has the answers and isn't willing to share them. He didn't elaborate on why."

"Oh my God." The look on Logan's face was animated. "After we confronted Alrik, we kept going, not turning back like I thought we would."

"Yes, I know. Alrik told me, and he was full of conspiracy theories about that, too."

"There's a cave. Hadrian had us all wait for him outside to keep watch, which, at the time, I didn't question. But now that I say it, I find it strange he didn't bring me with him."

"Why's that? You think he was doing something he didn't want you to see? Honestly, when Alrik told me you guys kept going north, I immediately thought Hadrian was taking you to the well. That he was going to fess up about knowing how to get home and maybe show you. At least, that's what I'd been hoping. But then we ran into each other, and you weren't acting like you'd just been given the answer. Actually, things felt tense. I thought maybe because I was out there alone, which worried you both, but I think there was more to it. Maybe Hadrian was worried I had reached Alrik and heard his side of things. You were also watching Hadrian strangely, and he was everywhere we were, like he didn't want us to talk. Frankly, I'm surprised he didn't curl up here between us to sleep."

"He told me at the cave that he stashed stuff in there from other-worldly trips. We'd used up a bunch of our firepower trying to get Alrik to release the clansmen, and Hadrian said he needed to restock. The whole thing was a waste of time if you ask me since the natives with Alrik clearly wanted to be there. None of them were willing to leave. We had no choice but to release Alrik and go."

"It's strange Hadrian would even attempt it, considering that, according to Alrik, the clansmen chose to be with him. Unless Hadrian thought they'd had a change of heart, and he wanted to assure them they'd be welcomed back with him?"

"Actually, yes, he did extend that invitation. I saw a lot of headshaking going on, though, and I knew they didn't want to leave. It was all very strange. Do the natives even know what Alrik is doing, what he's using them to do?"

"I don't know," I admitted. "So, you say Hadrian told you he kept supplies in that cave? Did he come out with anything? How long was he gone?"

"About an hour or so. And he took his sack in with him, and it looked heavier when he came out, so I'm guessing he did put stuff in there."

"Why would he stash ammo there and not here?"

"I'm sure he has it here as well. He could very well have stuff stashed strategically all over the place. But it made sense to me, considering we still had a long ride home ahead of us and barely any supplies. Alrik's group put up quite a struggle when we arrived. They didn't have explosives and I didn't see many weapons except some clubs and bows and arrows, and Alrik waved around a gun but didn't use it. Did you see him with the gun?"

"Yes, it was in his tent. I saw it there." It wasn't a complete lie. "I wonder why he didn't use it against you guys when you showed up?"

"He probably doesn't have a lot of bullets left, and he knew Hadrian would be unsuccessful in convincing the natives to leave. It made more sense to wing a few rocks and arrows at us."

"I hope no one was hurt when you guys clashed."

He shook his head. "No. We set off a few explosives around the perimeter to shake things up, but the natives didn't want to hurt each other, and we didn't want to see anyone get hurt either."

"That's a relief. It's strange, though, that Hadrian wanted to go there, all things considered. You'd think it'd just be a waste of his time and weapons?"

"You're thinking that wasn't the purpose of his trip there? That maybe the cave was his real destination?"

Now, I shrugged. "I dunno. Possibly. But I think he did want to see if any of the clan wanted to return. I do believe he was honest about that. But now I'm thinking about the cave and wondering if the well may be there?"

"Do you think it's possible to get home through the well?"

The sun was rising and began to light up the

interior of the cave. Self-consciously, I ran my fingers through my bedraggled hair. "I don't know. But I'm looking forward to us having a conversation with Hadrian about it."

"If there's a way home and he knows, he is going to tell us about it. One way or another," Logan vowed.

The icy, determined look on his face gave me a chill colder than my left hand ever had.

CHAPTER 12

The camp soon filled with sounds of the day getting started. Logan and I used a bowl of water and a couple of clean rags to scrub our faces and freshen up. We'd had to use short, peeled sticks to scrub at our teeth since our arrival — toothbrushes being one of the things Hadrian hadn't thought to grab from other worlds.

"Ready?" Logan asked, seeing me lace up my borrowed boots.

"Yes."

We'd discussed at length how we planned on talking to Hadrian. Instead of hurling accusations, we decided I would come clean about meeting Alrik and reveal what he'd accused him of. Then, hopefully, Hadrian would see the error of his ways and tell us all he knew. I couldn't help but hope and pray that today would be our last day here. If there was a way home, we'd leave and never look back.

We left the cave, descending the short distance

to the ground. I was careful, not wanting to risk a repeat injury. Seeing Hadrian at the fire pit, we headed in that direction. As we got closer, I could hear him talking to a handful of men and women, his speech blunt and using hand gestures to aid in his conversation. Seeing our approach, he gave a nod. It was clear by the sad faces and the weary expression on Hadrian's face they were discussing the ambush that cost two lives.

Respectfully, we waited until the group had finished their discussion before Logan asked Hadrian if we could speak privately.

The three of us headed over to the waterfall, distancing ourselves from the others.

"It's a sad day." Hadrian's face appeared drawn with worry and regret. He looked older to me.

"It is," Logan said while I nodded my head in agreement.

Hadrian's glance went from Logan to me, and he smiled tightly. "I guess you two have talked."

"We have, and I want to admit something," I began. "When you guys met up with me yesterday, I was on my way back from Alrik's campground." I didn't know what else to call it — there had been tents.

"So, you met him." It wasn't a question, more of a statement.

"Yeah, and he told me some things."

Hadrian suddenly didn't know what to do with

his hands, shoving them into his pockets, then pulling them out to wring them like they were cold. Seeing him act that way made me aware of my own hands and the secret I held.

Logan saw me watching Hadrian, and he met my gaze. "How about we go for a short walk?"

It was a good idea, just in case I had to reveal what I could do.

Hadrian shrugged as though it didn't matter to him, but I could see he was anxious to move. We walked toward the exit of the alcove that the settlement was located in. The high stone on either side of us made me feel secure but claustrophobic at the same time. If an attack came from above, like from those crazy huge birds, we'd be sitting ducks. However, it did provide protection from larger animals. Just outside the stone tunnel-like walkway, the area opened up again into vast green fields with ginormous trees.

Hadrian climbed onto a boulder and sat down while we took a seat on a pair of rocks facing him. He laughed uneasily. "Such serious faces. I can just imagine the lies Alrik spouted about me."

"Were they? Lies?" I asked.

Now, he frowned. "Payton, I hope you're smart enough to not believe the rantings of a power-hungry madman?"

"I haven't even told you what he said."

He grimaced. "Well, I can just imagine."

"You said he was making the natives build up the ruins into a temple to worship him," I began. When he said nothing, I continued. "Were you aware of the stone tablet with hieroglyphs?"

He nodded.

"He's digging for the well," I revealed, but he probably already knew that.

Now, he snorted. "He won't find it there."

"But you know where it is, don't you?" Logan charged. "In that cave? Is that why you made me wait for you outside with the others?"

Hadrian sighed. He looked across the land, avoiding eye contact and answering Logan's question.

"We know you can get home. You told Logan so, plus you practically said as much the first night we were here. Alrik believes you can. He also thinks you're keeping the details of how you do it to yourself. Why would you do that?"

"Alrik," he spat. "Saintly Alrik would have you believe I am the enemy."

"Then convince us that you're not," I said.

"That night, you asked me if I missed home, I said I did not. It's because my world is dying. Every breath is a struggle. There's barely any food or clean water. Disease is rampant."

"You said, 'Weren't you paying attention when

you came through?'. As though being lost was our fault," I insisted.

"I'm sorry I said that. I guess I was protecting you from the truth, which I'm sure Logan has told you by now."

"What? About the worlds rotating?" That was his secret?

"Yes."

"So you don't know how to get home?" Logan clarified.

Hadrian looked each of us in the eyes. "Why would I want to return to a world on the verge of extinction? My family is dead. My friends are dead. There's nothing for me there. I wanted to start over. Someplace I can do the most good. I know I don't belong here, not really, but I want to." He ran a hand over his face. "I'm sorry if Alrik filled your head with notions of getting home. Even if I could get home, I wouldn't."

"But you leave and come back when you like," I said. "How do you do that if the worlds rotate? How do you know you're going to find this world and not some other place when you come back through the doorway? Have you been into the well and seen the tunnels branching off the cavern? Do they not rotate there? Is that how you find your way?"

He shook his head. "Despite what that stone

tablet shows, there's nothing there. I know. I've tried to swim down into the depths of the well. It just goes on and on until you run out of air. There's no cavern waiting at the end. At least none that I've ever found. When I first arrived here, I found that hieroglyph and thought the same thing as Alrik. As for how I find my way back here, the worlds don't rotate immediately," he clarified.

To be honest, I'd suspected as much since Logan and I had gone through doorways, turned, and left, only to return again. But we'd done that within the timespan of moments, really. Hadrian's jaunts had been long enough to gather supplies and such. The fact that he'd attempted to swim down into the well and couldn't find the cavern could be explained. At least, I hoped it could. Since he obviously didn't want to go home, he most likely didn't try very hard. He probably gave up too soon.

Before I had a chance to voice my next question, Hadrian continued. "I don't know exactly how long I have. I do know it's generally under an hour." He pulled out a pocket watch attached to a slim silver chain. "If I keep it under that time, I've always made it back."

"Ah, so you time your trips?" I said, and he nodded. I wondered if there'd been times when he hadn't made it back and had been forced to look for this world.

Logan narrowed his eyes. "Why do I feel like there's more to this?"

Hadrian laughed without mirth and tucked away his watch. "I'm sorry you feel that way. Look, if both of you think I have some evil plan in mind, you're free to leave anytime. You know where the exit is. I can even provide an escort."

So he was calling our bluff. Though his story sounded truthful, and I did feel pity for him about his world, I was with Logan. Something didn't feel right.

"I don't know about you guys," Logan said. "But I'm starving." He climbed off the rock and began walking back toward the passageway. With one hard look at Hadrian, I climbed down and caught up to Logan. Whatever was going on, it was obvious we weren't going to discover it now. My right palm tingled with heat. Concentrating, I willed it to cool.

Hadrian wasn't the only one who was not willing to divulge secrets.

CHAPTER 13

After breakfast, Logan and I sat by the vacated communal firepit. Hadrian had opted to leave camp with a small group of men and women on foot. With them, the men carried spears, and the women wicker baskets. I guessed they were off to forage for fruits and other foods. We weren't invited to go along, but I doubted it was a deliberate snub.

"I'm curious he didn't ask us if we had any theories about the well. Like, there's a friggin' mural in stone illustrating the thing here. You think he'd realize it had some significance attached to it," Logan scoffed.

"Most likely, he just thinks the well was depicted as a way home. I doubt he has any other ideas about what else it could do—unlike Alrik, who I guess never shared his ideas with Hadrian. Hadrian must have come across other wells in the worlds he's visited."

"You'd think."

A giant insect landed on my leg, and I smacked it

off. I'd be so thrilled to leave this place. Logan munched on some dried meat he still had from breakfast. I'd swear a person could chew a piece of that stuff all day long.

"I'm okay with him not asking. Then I'd have to worry about keeping the gifts in each world a secret."

Swallowing hard, Logan replied, "Can you keep control of it though? You seemed to be having some trouble when we first saw you."

"I'm still getting used to it. It's tied to my emotions, unfortunately."

He was about to take another bite of the jerky, then opted to stuff it in his pocket instead. "So, what do you want to do? Do you want to leave?"

"No. I want to check out that cave and find the well."

"Then what? You don't plan on seeing Alrik again, do you?" he asked.

"I dunno. But if we can find the well, I want to climb down in there and see what happens." Hadrian hadn't denied that the well was in or near the cave. I was sure it must be there.

"Really? You think Hadrian was lying about not being able to reach the cavern?"

"Probably not. But I suspect he didn't try very hard. You heard him. He doesn't want to get home. Do you think he'll let us go to the cave without any trouble?"

He shrugged. "I'm not sure. Especially since he's already told us his descent attempt failed. He may be wondering why we're so interested, considering Alrik is too."

"Just imagine if we make it into the cavern and find the other tunnels. If the worlds don't rotate, even if we can't find home, maybe we can find the world like ours, where I was a genie."

Logan smiled, understanding my reasoning. "Then you could wish us home."

"That's not all I'd do. I'd wish everyone home, then wish those wells into oblivion. Destroy them all, in every world."

"If Hadrian goes home, he'll die," Logan reminded me.

"So he says. Right now, he's lying to us about something. Maybe he's lying about that as well. Besides," I said, pushing my guilt aside, "None of us belong anywhere but our own worlds. Good or bad."

"It's kind of a moot point, though. If you wished the wells away, then maybe the gifts would no longer work. It'd be a risk. We could find ourselves trapped there in the alternate version of our world forever."

I hadn't thought that far ahead. It's not like I'd be able to wish us home first because the genie power wouldn't work then, so I'd not be able to destroy the wells. But if I destroyed the wells first, and possibly my genie power along with it, then we could be trapped, like Logan said. Unless destroying the wells automatically sent everyone back where they belonged? The whole thing gave me a headache.

Sudden loud wailing made us jump to our feet.

"Who is that? What's wrong?" I asked, my gaze frantically darting all around.

Logan did the same until our sights settled on a small gathering of women. They were looking around and calling out the same word, "Lucan, Lucan!" One of them was crying out the loudest.

We hurried over to them and tried to make sense of what they were saying.

One of the women pointed at a group of children who'd been playing, but now all stood stock still in fear.

"Logan, Lucan must be a child. She's lost her child."

"What? Where?" he asked.

Now, the same woman was gesturing toward the rock tunnel-like passageway.

"Oh no. I think she's trying to tell us that he followed Hadrian and the others," I surmised.

Logan put his hand on the arm of the wailing woman, attempting to gain her attention. "We go," he said. "We find." He also mimed his intentions until the woman nodded swiftly in understanding.

Just as we began jogging toward the passageway, Hadrian burst forward. Hot on his heels was the group he'd left with.

"Take cover! Into the caves!" he bellowed, waving his arms around dramatically.

Everyone scattered, scrambling to get to the safety of the caves. Logan joined Hadrian in helping to lift the terrified children and women up first. Loud screams overhead caused the clan to wail in fear.

Mesmerized by the sight in the sky, I stood several feet from the caves where I'd been ushering others forward to safety. Now I saw what had caused the panic.

"Payton!" Logan yelled, attempting to break the spell I found myself in.

Then, I felt myself physically shaken, and the spell was broken. "What is that?"

Logan's gaze joined mine, staring at the huge black cloud moving in. But it wasn't a cloud. It was a mass of birds.

"Get inside! Light your fires," hollered Hadrian toward the caves. "It's a swarm," he called out as he moved over to join us. "There isn't much time."

"Are those the birds that attacked us before?" I wasn't sure I wanted to know. With Logan's help and the use of fire and ice balls, we'd scared that other bird off. The look of rage on its face had promised revenge. Now, it appeared to have gathered its friends and returned to finish the job.

The three of us, with Hadrian's urging, scrambled into his cave, which was closest to us. Hadrian bent down and used a flint to spark up the kindling in his mini firepit. Before I could offer my services, I saw bright sparks and then a strong flame leap up to feed on the twigs and moss. Hadrian nurtured the fire until it shone bright and hot.

The view outside the cave went from light to dark, the swarm so large it blocked the sun.

"Damn it," Hadrian swore. "I should have known they'd return. Those birds, they're uncannily smart and have an ability to remember faces."

"Like crows," Logan said.

Over the squawks of the birds and the frightened cries from the tribe, and the horses and other animals left outside vulnerable, I could distinguish a wail of a woman.

"Oh, no! Logan. Lucan. The child."

Hadrian looked back at me over his shoulder. "Lucan? What about him?"

"Just before you came back, his mom was frantic. She was gesturing at the passageway, and we figured he'd snuck out and followed you," I informed him.

"We were on our way to search when you came running back. Did you have him with you?" Logan finished.

Hadrian shook his head. "No, I never saw him. He's young, about nine or ten. He should have enough sense to hide if he saw the threat."

That didn't make me feel better. Not when I could still make out the heartbreaking cries of his mother.

"There's nothing we can do right now. We'll just have to wait till the threat passes," Hadrian said. He had a sick, troubled look on his face that solidified my resolve.

"There's something we can do," I said, looking at Logan.

"Don't do it. We had enough trouble with one of those things, never mind a flock of 'em," Logan insisted.

"What are you talking about. Going out there now would be suicide." Hadrian nodded toward the giant birds, some of which had landed and stalked around the clearing. "You'd need a flame thrower."

I stared at Logan, who shook his head, and then I turned to Hadrian. "Well, it's a good thing I have one."

Before either of them had a chance to say another word, I bolted to the entrance and darted around the fire before jumping the few feet to the ground.

CHAPTER 14

As I knew he would, Logan landed beside me within seconds. To his credit, Hadrian followed next.

"What are you doing?" Hadrian demanded. "Both of you have a death wish!"

"Then go back to your cave!" My fear and anger ignited both hands simultaneously. One became a flaming torch, the other, blue with cold, dropping wet flakes of snow. Seeing my sudden display, Hadrian took a few steps back, his mouth hanging wide.

"What are you?" His words were barely audible.

Logan's gaze was everywhere, his stance, ready for battle. "Go back to your cave," he repeated my words to Hadrian. "We're going to search for Lucan."

Without missing a beat, Logan caught the snowballs I tossed at him and drilled them at the advancing birds. Getting hit square in the beak, one of them squawked its outrage and flew off.

"Can you throw the fire as well?" Hadrian

shouted over the loud squawks as more birds got blasted with snow.

I nodded affirmative. Turning my attention to my fiery palm, I focused on flinging fireballs. After a couple of times, I began with the snow again. It took a bit of maneuvering before I got it, the motions requiring rhythm since I had both hands waving — one throwing fire, the other, snow. It took concentration in order to keep lobbing snowballs toward the guys — Hadrian having joined in the fray — worrying I would mess up and throw fire at them instead. We advanced, moving slowly but surely in the direction of the passageway. All of us searched the area with our gazes, desperate for a glance of the missing boy.

Finally reaching our destination, we bolted down the length of the passage, meeting minimal threats. At the base of the rocks where the three of us had gathered earlier, we saw Lucan crouched in fear. More of the huge birds glided overhead and sat perched on guard. Seeing us hurry toward the boy, several let loose angry squawks of protest. No doubt they thought we attempted to escape their ambush.

One of the birds landed almost right on top of us, knocking me down. As it flapped its wings, sending up a torrent of dirt, pebbles, small sticks, and grass, I heard a crack and saw its head jerk back. Logan stood in front of me now, and though I hadn't seen what he'd done, I had a feeling he'd kicked its beak. Feathers ruffled, and it shook its head, causing some of them to cascade to the ground beside me. The sheer size of a single feather was incredible, like looking at a palm frond.

Lucan cried out, and I could hear Hadrian consoling him.

"We'll distract them. You get Lucan back toward the caves, and we'll be right behind you," Logan shouted, knowing we faced threats on both fronts.

The bird he kicked was advancing again. Behind it, two others landed, flanking it. In that moment I wished Hadrian had thought to bring a gun with him. Would have helped even the odds a bit.

Getting up into a crouching position, I was able to look back and see Hadrian scoop up the boy in his arms. Tucking down his head, he suddenly bolted in the direction of the passageway. Two of the birds immediately took after him while the first one remained, having an axe to grind with Logan.

Standing now, I detoured around Logan as he and the bird squared off. Then I dashed toward the other two birds. More circled around overhead, their shadows flashing against the rocks and grass. Trying to gain the attention of the two birds pursuing Hadrian and Lucan, I kept pausing to whip snowballs at their backsides. Finally, one of them stopped and spun around. Catching me off guard with its swift change of direction, I almost ran right into it. Taking three steps, it was in front of me, and I got an up-close view of the shine of its huge breast as its head pulled up and back. I knew it was attempting to gain momentum to surge down and peck me. Just before its head began its descent, I shoved my icy palm against its throat, burying it where the feathers were thin. The bird froze, I thought in shock but then realized as I stepped back and watched the eyes, now clearly visible, glassed over. Then it fell to its side, legs, and feet hard and straight.

"Holy sh−" I only had a moment to stare in shock before Lucan's screams cut into my daze.

A flock of angry fowl had descended from above, focused on the pair, and even blocked the entrance to the passage. Besieged, Hadrian had dropped down and crouched overtop Lucan, using his body to shield the boy.

Logan came up beside me, having dealt with his own issue. "Okay?" I asked him.

He nodded, his face twisted with anger and frustration at the sight before us. "I don't know what to do. There's so many. They just keep coming."

His voice sounded defeated, and that enraged me more.

Our saving grace came from the unlikeliest of places. A pair of massive T-Rexes came into view, heading fast in our direction. The flock of birds appeared to have gained their attention.

"Oh great," Logan groaned. But then he, too, realized our good fortune. The birds, seeing the threat, squawked and took off, our presence all but forgotten.

But now we faced a new predator. "Run, run!" Logan and I hollered, barreling toward Hadrian and Lucan.

Hadrian leapt up, scooped Lucan into his arms again, and we all raced into the passageway.

When we burst into the clearing, Hadrian began shouting, warning the others of the new threat. "Go," he told Lucan, directing him toward his cave and the anxious arms of his mother.

The three of us kept a wary eye overhead. The birds were gone, but we worried the dinos would find a way into our sanctuary.

"Have they ever breached the area before?" Logan asked.

Hadrian shook his head. "Not that I've witnessed, but I can't say for sure."

"Will we be safe in the caves if they get in?" I asked, my voice loud to be heard over the ungodly roars of the giant beasts.

Hadrian, now that the first threat had passed, looked at me, his gaze wandering down to my hands and lingering there as he spoke. "Even you wouldn't stand a chance against them. Their skin is like armor. We should be safe in the caves."

The way he'd appraised me, a mixture of calculation and anxiousness, concerned me. Would he connect the well with the presence of my powers?

One threat at a time.

Scrambling, we all climbed into Hadrian's cave, going as deep as it allowed. The small fire at the entrance still burned, but I feared it would do little to deter a T-Rex if it decided to shove its head inside. Leaning against the back wall, our eyes remained glued to the clearing outside.

"Do you have special powers as well?" Hadrian asked Logan, his tone laced with the bitterness of betrayal.

Before Logan could deny the possession of any powers, I answered for him. "Logan is a champion fighter."

Hadrian's appraising gaze swept Logan's taller form. "Really?" His tone was tinged in doubt.

"My ability comes from discipline and hard work," Logan said. "Years of training."

Now Hadrian's gaze flashed to me. "And what of your ability, Payton? I hardly think what I saw comes from training?"

I shrugged. "It takes some practice. I'm still working on it."

He snorted and shook his head. "And let me ask you something else." His voice became quieter since the dino's roars seemed to be growing fainter. "Did you have this ability before you arrived here?"

If I lied, I had a feeling he'd see through me. Logan and I exchanged a look.

"To be honest, I never noticed it before." Let him do with that as he wished.

Before we could continue our conversation, Lucan appeared. Arms waving and excited chatter coming from his mouth, he moved around the fire and rushed into the cave. A few others followed. The relief and smiles on their faces were contagious. Apparently, the threat had passed. As we left the cave, Hadrian shot Logan and I each a look of warning. Feeling subdued, we followed, knowing things between us were far from over.

CHAPTER 15

The safe recovery of Lucan, combined with thwarting the bird attack, made for a festive vibe around camp that evening. The bonfire loomed high, and the smell of meat flooded the air. Hadrian, Logan, and I all received congratulatory pats on the back and what I took to be hearty praise over our successes of the day. There were no displays of fear or uncertainty—at least that I was aware of—in regard to my shocking abilities. Although, I supposed our victory outweighed any reservations the tribe might have about my gifts. I didn't try to console myself with hopes that no one had seen what I'd done. And yet, fires had been lit at the entryway of the caves, and the tribe members had no doubt been deep inside, putting as much distance between themselves and the birds as possible. So, maybe, I allowed, if they'd seen me in action, at best, their view had been hindered by smoke and flames by their own fires. And just maybe, no one had seen me at all.

But Lucan had. There was no getting around that fact. He must have. Even though his head had been tucked low against Hadrian for protection, he had to have caught a glimpse of me throwing balls of fire and snow? He could tell others. Would they believe the boy? He had been scared. And things had happened quickly.

Every time Hadrian turned his gaze on me, I couldn't help but shiver. I knew another reckoning was looming. The thought of Alrik entered my mind. He'd awed the tribe with little tricks, making them believe he possessed god-like powers. For that, he'd earned banishment. Would that be our fate as well? Logan and I hadn't had the chance to discuss what we would reveal about my gifts. I was determined, however, that if secrets were being spilled tonight, ours wouldn't be the only ones.

Side by side, Logan and I sat holding crudely made dishes. We both had a bit of meat and weird vegetables, along with cool water for dinner. Logan's appetite appeared to be as lacking as mine for a change, surprising since, generally, nothing discouraged his hunger. His and Hadrian's exchange of icy glances across the leaping flames no doubt led to the anomaly.

Finally, late into the evening, the others slowly wandered off to their beds, leaving the three of us alone. Hadrian rose and joined us, and we all sat in uneasy silence.

"I think it's time Payton and I left," Logan began.

Hadrian visibly bristled. "Don't get ahead of yourselves. Do you really want to go back into the tunnels, ending up who knows where, endlessly searching for home?"

"It doesn't have to be that way, though, does it?" I insisted.

"At least here, you know what you're getting. Yes, it's dangerous and unpredictable, but you're not alone." He ignored my question.

"I'm surprised you're not anxious to see us leave," Logan said. "You haven't exactly been exerting warm and fuzzy vibes lately."

Hadrian's look hardened. "We have some things to work through. I'd prefer you both stay, and we can learn to trust each other."

"Good. You start," I said.

He shook his head in frustration. "You both seem to think I'm withholding information. I'm not. I've told you what I know. Unlike you two."

"In the morning, Payton and I are leaving. We don't require an escort. As you saw, we're equipped to take care of ourselves," Logan said, wearing a stubborn look on his face.

Hadrian, clearly disappointed, shrugged. "Fine.

Suit yourselves. You're not prisoners here. You're guests. And despite our differences, I appreciate your help today. Things could have gone badly if it weren't for you two."

Judging by Logan's face, he was unmoved by the praise.

"Thanks," I said. "Happy to help."

Hadrian rose suddenly. "It's been a long day. I'm going to bed. I hope you'll stay long enough to say goodbye to all of us." Not waiting for a reply, he left.

As soon as he was out of sight, Logan rose as well. I followed suit. The fire was still bright enough to see the way to our cave. We made ourselves comfortable in the furs and, exhausted, soon fell asleep.

When I woke up in the morning, it took me a while to sit up. When I did, I felt dizzy and heavy. My mouth was dry, and my sight was blurry. I reached out for Logan and found the space where he should be empty.

"He's gone," came a voice.

"Hadrian?" I squinted at the mouth of the cave and saw a shadowy shape there.

Closer he came and then knelt at the side of the furs. "Payton, don't try to get up. Something was wrong with the water, I think. A bunch of us are down. Or it could have been the meat."

I ran a hand over my face and felt around for the

canteen. Sounds of scuffling were followed by the feel
of the leather flagon being passed into my hands. He
took a moment to unscrew the cap and helped guide it
to my parched lips.

"I don't feel so good," I told him.

"I don't feel great either," he admitted.

I took a few sips of the water and passed the
canteen back to him. "Logan?" I asked.

"He's okay. He's sick, like the rest of us, but he
made it outside."

Why wouldn't he have woken me? At least to
see if I was okay. Something didn't make sense, but my
head was so cloudy and confused that I couldn't figure
things out.

I felt Hadrian's hands gently guide me back to
the furs. "Rest," he said.

Yeah, right. Watching him move toward the exit,
I struggled again to sit up as soon as he left. I had to
crawl on all fours, snagging the canteen and pulling
the strap over my head along the way to follow him.
Getting the few feet to the ground would require some
skill. Sadly, at the moment, I was lacking even the
basic ability to stand and walk at the same time. If I
could spin around and go down feet first, that might
do it, I figured. Awkwardly, I made my descent slowly
and carefully, releasing a breath I'd held when my feet
touched down. Though my sight was still blurred, I

could hear scrambling, retching, groaning, and faint cries all around the vicinity.

Hadrian hadn't been kidding about everyone being sick. What could have caused this? I struggled to make sense of what he'd said. The water, or the meat? Had he meant it'd been somehow tainted? Bad or poisoned?

"Payton, you shouldn't be up. You look like hell." That was Logan's voice, sounding distressed but strong. Relief lit through me.

My hands reached out to grasp him, clinging like a lifeline. "Logan? Are you all right? Hadrian said you were sick. That everyone is sick."

"Including you." His grip on my arms was solid, comforting. He led me a-ways, and soon I was lowering again to soft furs. He jostled me a bit as he removed the strap from over my head and set the canteen aside. Fighting the urge to sleep, I struggled against his now gentle hands, smoothing my brow.

"Rest," he soothed.

Had we climbed back up to our cave? I couldn't recall. How could I feel so ill when I'd barely eaten? Neither of us had had an appetite, but I did recall drinking quite a bit last night. Soon after I'd fallen asleep, I'd been awakened by the urge to tinkle, and I'd had to scale down the stone and wander off into the brush. After returning to the furs, I recalled nothing.

Nothing except weird dreams and pain in my belly.

CHAPTER 16

"How can you still be moving?" I asked Logan, who'd briefly laid down at my side. "Did you bring us to Hadrian's cave?" My befuddled head ached too much to look around.

"I dunno, and yes, I did," he answered. "I guess I didn't get as much in my system."

I ran a hand over my face. No fever, but I was shaky and clammy. "I wonder what happened?"

"Maybe one of the birds shat in the water? Bird flu or something?"

I tried to shrug, but it hurt. "Maybe."

"Hadrian seems okay, like me. But come to think of it, I didn't drink much from my cup, mostly from my canteen. He was probably the same." They must have filled their canteens before the water-tainting incident then. If that was what had happened. I'd drank a few cup-fulls of water. That must have been it. Especially since I distinctly recalled Hadrian had a mouthful of food every time we'd looked at each other. So it most likely wasn't the meat.

Logan sighed loudly and moved slowly, getting up. "I'll be back to check on you. I have to help the others. Hadrian's doing that now, but he'll need help."

My hands grasped his pant leg. I knew he was right, but I didn't want him to leave me alone. "Don't be long, okay?"

Awkwardly, he bent down and kissed my forehead. "I'll be close. Just call out if you need me. Try and rest."

Attempting to be brave, I nodded and released him. "Okay. I'm really weak and tired."

It was a while before I felt someone by my side again.

It took only a moment to realize it wasn't Logan.

Cold hands rooted around my head and neck, and then something around my throat tightened like they were trying to choke me.

"Hey, geddoff!" I croaked, struggling pitifully. "Geddoff me!"

As my hands stirred to life, one slightly warm, one slightly cool—as though igniting fully was too much effort—something gave way. Like the chord, my assailant used broke, and the pressure on my neck disappeared. The sudden release caused me to fall back onto the furs again, and both my hands fizzled out. The shadowy shape slunk away to the exit, taking advantage of my weakened state. Whoever it was knew I couldn't give chase.

I could yell, though.

"Logan! Logan!"

He barreled into the cave seconds later. I was trying to sit up at this point and reaching around my neck, which had begun to ache. And to my mortification, I was crying in misery.

Logan's arms came around me, holding me close. He even rocked me gently like a child. "It's okay, I'm here," he crooned.

"Someone was here. They…they…choking me," I said between sobs.

He froze. "What? What do you mean? Are you sure?" His voice was deadly cold.

"Uh-huh." I nodded, wiping my nose against his chest.

"Lemme go look. I'll be right back," he added as my hands fisted his shirt. He pried me loose and was gone. I laid back on the furs, sniffling. Why would someone try and hurt me? My recent actions hadn't warranted an attack. I'd helped when there was danger. I'd aided in saving Lucan.

Thinking back, I attempted to piece together what I'd felt. Cold hands. Around my neck. *Searching…* Maybe they'd been after something? But what? I didn't have anything of value. No necklace of gold, no pendant dangling on a chain.

But wait.

I did have something of value around my neck.

The cobwebs in my brain began to break apart, and things began to clear.

My flash drive.

I'd worn it for so long I'd practically forgotten about it.

But why? Why would someone want that? There was no electricity here. No laptop to plug it into. And anyway, what did it contain but the stories of a girl's journeys. Fantastical journeys. Who would be interested in something like...

Alrik.

Of course. He'd be interested. Very interested, in fact.

And now, as the remnants of clarity returned to me, pushing away the clouds of confusion with laser determination, I knew.

It had to be him. Him with all his questions.

And me, fool that I had been, had delivered to him my own handwritten journal with all the facts about the well.

And the gifts.

Logan returned to the cave. "There's no one. Nothing."

Of course, there wasn't. Alrik had no doubt scurried away fast like the spider he was. "My bag. In our cave. Please, Logan. Bring it to me."

He nodded once and left.

But I already knew. Alrik had found my journal and read it. And now he'd returned for more information from my flash drive. He'd known about it because of the journal.

When Logan returned, he put the pack in front of me. A quick search revealed what I already knew.

The journal was gone.

And now, so was my flash drive.

"What is it, Payton? What's going on?"

Bleakly, I stared into Logan's eyes. "I brought my journal when I went searching for you guys."

"Okay."

"And it's gone. I think—no, I'm sure—Alrik has it."

Logan slumped down beside me. "You're positive? You couldn't have lost it—"

"No," I interrupted. "He has it. I'm sure. He had so many questions about the well and other worlds I'd been to. And then he just let me go. Come back, he told me, when I figured out that Hadrian's been lying to me. But he's read the journal, and he knows I wasn't telling him everything."

"What was written in it?" He wore a sick look

on his face, and I felt guilty for putting it there.

"Everything. At least all the stuff about that last world where we thought we were home. Where the feds were after us. And all the stuff we learned about the well."

He groaned, and I knew it wasn't just because of the bad water.

"I think he came back to get the flash drive, though fat lot of good it's gonna do him with no electricity."

Logan shrugged. "He's resourceful. Who's to say he doesn't have a few batteries stashed?"

"It's possible. It would explain why he went to all this trouble to take it," I said.

"Why not just ask for it? Didn't you leave on good terms?"

"Yeah, but if he read the journal, he'd know I didn't tell him about the well. He wasn't going to risk I was keeping more secrets from him."

Logan clenched his fists in anger.

Before he could begin a tirade, Hadrian entered the cave. "Is everything okay? I saw you rush in here and then back out, is Payton..." He stopped when he saw me sitting up.

"I'm okay," I said.

He ran a weary hand over his pale face. Obviously, looking at him, he was exhausted and still not feeling well.

"You warned everyone not to drink from the well? And dump your canteens if you filled them again last night," I said.

"Yeah, already on it," Logan assured me.

"If everything's okay, can you come and help me again?" Hadrian asked Logan.

Logan and I exchanged glances, and then they left. Now wasn't the time to explain theories to Hadrian. I knew it would take everything in Logan to not ride off pell-mell and confront Alrik. He'd done a foolish, cruel thing to these kind, innocent people, and there was going to be hell to pay.

CHAPTER 17

It took hours for me to begin to feel better. Not until evening did I attempt to stir from Hadrian's cave and shuffle to the communal firepit. A few other stragglers gathered there, none looking any better than I felt. Overhead, a wide black sky filled with twinkling stars. Between the intoxicating fresh air and the whiff of campfire smoke, if I closed my eyes, I could almost imagine I was up north at our cottage. The wave of nostalgia nearly knocked me off my shaky legs. Down, I pushed the memories of home, of family.

A big pot of what I soon saw was broth bubbled away when a wooden bowl passed into my shaky hands. I nodded my thanks to the ancient woman who looked to be standing strong. Earlier in the day, Hadrian had gone off with two spare horses to carry back jugs of water. When Logan told me about it during one of his quick visits, we figured he'd gone to that creek we'd found upon entry to this world. Its distance hopefully assured the water's safety. The pond here would probably be fine to drink from again soon, considering the fresh supply it had via the running stream and waterfall.

Logan had also mentioned he'd not told Hadrian of our suspicions about Alrik. We opted to wait, considering it might be better to deal with Alrik on our own.

"If you're up to it, we can leave in the morning," Logan said to me quietly as he sat down at my side with his own bowl of broth.

"If we're both up to it." He looked terrible, and it wasn't the first time I wished I'd possessed the healing touch again.

Hadrian had returned, and I saw him making rounds in the camp, continuing to check on the others. Seeing his dedication made me feel somewhat guilty over the suspicions that had crept into my addled head as I'd tossed and turned throughout the day.

When he joined us at the fire, he stayed long enough for him and Logan to finish up their bowls of broth, and then they both went back to caring for the others.

Later that night, when I was curled up in our own furs, Logan returned just as the moon became visible through the mouth of the cave. He settled in beside me, and his hand reached for mine.

"How're you doing?" I asked, garnering a long sigh in response. "That good, eh?"

"I'll be okay after some sleep," he assured me.

"I've been wondering," I began.

"About what?"

"About Hadrian. Do you think I was too quick to blame Alrik for today?"

Logan rolled on his side so we were face to face. "Do you believe you were wrong?"

"I dunno. I've had time to think, and it seemed kind of weird that just last night, we told Hadrian we planned to leave in the morning."

Logan closed his eyes, and I knew he was gathering his patience.

"We already figured Hadrian hasn't been truthful with us about the well. Also, he may have been magnanimous about us leaving to our faces, but..."

"But, he may want us to remain," Logan continued.

"Watching him tonight, though, I feel almost bad saying this out loud, never mind thinking it. He was really concerned over everyone's welfare. You must have noticed that."

He yawned and ran a hand over his face. "Yeah, Hadrian always seems very concerned about everyone. But is it concern or guilt? Who knows what's going on in his head? My dad always said sociopaths make excellent actors."

"You think he's…"

"Shhh. I've no idea. The only person I truly know is you. Alrik could be the sociopath." His voice was low.

"Or desperate—both of them. How do we know who to trust?"

He squeezed my hand in affection. "We don't trust anyone but each other. Easier that way."

As his eyes closed and his breathing became rhythmic, I knew he was right.

***

The next morning, we were gone before anyone woke. We went on foot so as not to have to worry about what to do with one or more horses once we got to our destination. It would take longer, but it couldn't be helped. I felt bad about not saying goodbye. We'd each packed a sack full of supplies and gauged our timeline to be at least doubled. Alrik's camp was our destination. We planned to confront him and see if he was responsible for yesterday's calamity.

The alternative would be unsettling.

"How do we know if he's lying?"

Logan was looking behind us again, seeing if any followed. "I dunno. If he is a sociopath, it'll be next to impossible to tell."

"He didn't seem to me to be the calm, cool, and

collected kind. His emotions were all over the place. At least, until we talked at the end—before he let me leave."

"Maybe we should come up with a plan. Like play dumb, you know. Say that Hadrian is a liar, and we had to leave 'cause he tried to poison us." He looked back again. At this rate, he was going to have a sore neck after a few hours.

"Maybe instead, we ought to just bypass him altogether and head directly to the cave and hopefully the well."

"But he has your stuff," Logan argued.

"Does he? Do we know for sure? We didn't get a chance to search Hadrian's cave. I wish I'd have thought to when I was in it." I hadn't exactly been in my right mind at the time. Plus, by the time I could stay upright, the light had been dimming, and I would have probably torched the place if I'd lit my palm.

"If he took the flash drive, he could have stashed it anywhere. And I highly doubt it would have been in his cave, considering he had to make a quick getaway."

"True. He'd hardly pause to hide it in his own cave where I was staying," I said.

"No. That wouldn't make sense. Besides, you said you suspect Alrik of taking your journal when you were detained."

"Yes. And whoever took the journal, it would

only make sense that they would also take the flash drive. Otherwise, how else would they know about it."

"Also true."

"Anyway, I don't really care. All I want to do is get home. Then, I can rewrite everything." The thought of home washed over me again, and once more, I pushed it back down.

"Payton, I know you're pinning a lot of hope on that hieroglyph. That the tethers will bring us home. But it may not be the case."

I didn't want to consider the possibility of defeat. "Don't you think it's strange that Alrik would be so close to the cave where the well is all this time and still not have found it? You'd think the natives would know about it," I changed the subject.

"They may not even know what it is he has them looking for," he said, letting me have my way. "The language barrier and all."

"It's so ironic, don't you think? What he's been searching for is so close, and he has no idea."

I had to wonder if all this time, all the wells we'd seen and passed by, could the doorway home have been right there all along?

That would really be ironic.

CHAPTER 18

After two days and almost an entire night of hard walking, we reached Alrik's camp as the sun was going down. Just like when I'd been here before, we crouched in the brush, spying on the camp. This time, the growing darkness also helped to cloak our presence. Natives were still out amongst the ruins, working away with their crude picks and shovels, using wooden buckets to haul away dirt. Alrik himself cruised around the area, head held arrogantly high, black cape fluttering around his ankles in the slight breeze.

"The moment of truth," Logan pronounced dramatically.

"Yeah, yeah."

Another few minutes passed. "What do you want to do? Confront him, or search the cave?"

While I was deciding, the choice was taken from me.

"There you are!" a hiss came from the shadows

behind us.

We both spun around to face Hadrian.

He was alone, at least, from what I could see.

Keeping low, we all scrambled back from our hiding spot. Once far enough away, we stared daggers at each other.

"What are you doing?" Hadrian demanded.

"Isn't it obvious?" I said with a snort.

"Actually, no, it isn't. What it appears is that you're going after Alrik. Alone. Which is foolish no matter what powers you have."

He watched as Logan and I exchanged glances.

"Unless...you're deciding whether to bypass him and go straight to the cave?"

Were we that obvious?

Logan stared at him defiantly. "Whatever we decide, it's our business. Unless you're here to try and stop us. Then, we're going to have a problem."

Hadrian shook his head and smiled grimly. "When did I become the enemy?"

After looking at us a bit longer, his expression hardened. "Wait a minute. You think I could be the one who poisoned everyone. You're not sure, is that it?" he charged.

"Convince us it wasn't you," Logan said.

When Hadrian continued to stare at us with his mouth hanging open, I put my opinion forward.

"Right after we tell you we're leaving, it happened."
I saw him about to object, and I rushed to continue.
"Honestly, I—well, both of us—don't think you'd
stoop so low as to treat the tribe as collateral damage
just to get at us."

"Unless…" Logan said ominously.

"Unless what?" Hadrian charged.

"Unless what Arik said to Payton was right.
That you're keeping us here for some reason."

Hadrian shook his head. "I'm not. The only way
to prove it to you is to back you up. What do you want
to do? Alrik or the cave?"

Watching the defeat on Hadrian's face, I again
feared we'd misjudged him. But also, I couldn't be
sure. I'd never met anyone so hard to read in my life.

"Let's bypass Alrik and go to the cave," I said.
"It's late. I'm tired, and I don't feel like getting into it
with anyone." If things went the way I hoped, I'd be
sleeping in my own bed tonight.

Taking a wide detour around Alrik's camp, we
continued north. Hadrian had brought a horse with
him, not his fancy white one, but one of the sturdy
brown ones from this world. I guess if you were trying
to be stealthy, a huge white horse might draw attention.
Hadrian held the animal by its reins, opting to walk
alongside Logan and me.

"How far is it?" I hadn't been lying when I

said I was tired. However, the thought of the cave, and possibly the well, and the dangling hope of home spurred me on.

"Not far," Hadrian assured me.

"You don't need to stay," Logan told him. "We can figure things out from here."

Hadrian's sigh was dramatic. "I take it you're hoping the well is in the cave. Am I right?"

When neither Logan nor I said anything, Hadrian continued. "The well isn't in the cave. However, you need to go through it to access the well."

"Come to think of it," I pondered. "The hieroglyph didn't show the well as being enclosed. That's probably why Alrik wasn't searching there."

"Precisely," Hadrian agreed. "And even if he'd entered the cave — it's actually a vast system of caves — he probably wouldn't have found the well."

"It's that hard to find?" I asked him.

He shrugged. "Not if you know where to look."

"The caves are about an hour or so from Alrik's camp, from what I recall," Logan said. He looked at me. "Are you up for that?"

Now, it was my turn to shrug and sigh dramatically. "I suppose."

"We could always make camp," Hadrian suggested. "But considering you two think I may be the bad guy here, I think we should just push through."

"Good idea." Logan didn't bother to offer him any assurances he was mistaken.

We still felt on edge. I know I did. And the way Logan kept Hadrian in his sights and a careful eye on our surroundings, relayed his thoughts.

"How is everyone at camp? All recovered?" I asked.

"Yes, doesn't appear to be any lingering effects," Hadrian answered. "If you two plan on diving into the well and trying your luck, then I will confront Alrik."

"On your own?" Logan said with disbelief. "Didn't you just lecture us about it?"

"Yeah, and you hardly have a built-in arsenal," I reminded him. I was relieved he didn't tell us we were wasting our time with the well. Hope was what was keeping me going.

"No. But I do have one stashed in the cave," he said. "Despite you two thinking I may have done that to my own clan, I know it was Alrik. I know him, and I know what he's capable of. He had a score to settle with me for coming here, and he hoped to get even. Though it surprises me that even he would stoop so low. There are women and children at camp. Someone could have died."

Again, that gnawing in my belly made me feel we'd misjudged him, but at the same time, the little nagging voice in my head warned me to tread carefully.

If Alrik had been the one to taint the well, then I knew Hadrian hadn't been the target. I had. I'd been the one to take my journal with me to search for the guys and then not notice it missing. I couldn't be one hundred percent sure, though, that Alrik had been the one to take it. Just as easily, it could have been Hadrian. Just as I didn't know who now had my flash drive. Either one of them had opportunity and motive. The scary thing was if it was Hadrian, then what did he hope to gain? Alrik—I knew his end game was always to figure out a way home. Plus, he had no reason to trust me or anyone else. And he was already suspicious of Hadrian.

But if Hadrain had taken the journal, and then the flash drive, what did he want to learn? Had he wanted to know about the well and the gifts, just like Alrik? If so, why not just ask us?

Logan was right to be on guard.

We were in a strange world, surrounded by threats.

Some were possibly much closer than we liked.

CHAPTER 19

It was full on dark by the time we reached the cave. The mouth of the opening, about the height of Logan and maybe four feet across, yawned before us, beckoning us onward into its dark depth.

The guys each sparked a flint and lit a torch placed strategically in the brush beside the cave's entrance.

"Ready?" Logan asked me.

"As I'll ever be." I knew I sounded foreboding, but I had a lot riding on this hunch, and things hadn't exactly worked out so great for us in the past.

Logan gestured to Hadrian. "Lead on."

Hadrian entered the cave, the inky blackness swallowing him up except for the beacon of light from his torch. Logan looked at me and smiled, attempting to soften the moment. I entered next, leaving Logan to follow.

"Stay close," Hadrian instructed. "The path is

winding and a bit tricky."

Glancing down at the irregular dirt floor, I didn't notice any path or trail of any kind. I guessed he was speaking figuratively. "Is it far?"

"No. Just a few minutes."

The torchlight bounced off the cave walls and illuminated the high ceiling. Once we'd entered within, the entire area opened up into long twisting tunnels that reminded me of another more familiar labyrinth. We also passed hollowed out areas that could pass for rooms, and I wondered if anyone, like the clan's ancestors, had once called this place home.

Dangling vines hung over what I soon saw was an exit when Hadrian pushed them aside, and the dark night and starry sky came into view.

"It's here," he said, his voice low as though entering upon some sacred place.

Logan and I soon stood at his side, and together, we approached the well.

I felt uneasy suddenly, as though this were the moment of truth. Would Hadrian now demand answers to long held questions about the well? Not that I knew all the answers, but enough to make him or perhaps many others covet the enticing secrets it held.

Hadrian stared down at his feet.

A moment later, he broke the silence. "I...I wish you would stay. But I understand, maybe more than anyone how it is to long for home."

To me, this sounded so final. As though Hadrian thought we were parting ways forever. And yet, he'd assured us the well was nothing but a death trap. Just as I was about to question him, another voice pierced the darkness.

"Then why don't you return?"

All of us started and stared in the direction of the voice. Alrik emerged from the brush.

"What? How?" Hadrian sputtered.

"I knew you'd return. And I was ready and waiting," he said, his tone practically gleeful. My spies alerted me to your presence."

I assumed he meant that he'd set a few of the natives on guard patrol.

Alrik's gaze met mine, and a shiver ran over me. No wonder I'd had such a terrible feeling. Staring at him now in the surrounding darkness, wearing that twisted, triumphant look on his face, he reminded me so much of Lord Nelson.

"You thought you were so smart. All of you. It's why you didn't care that I dug and dug so endlessly, searching. You knew all along what it was I looked for, and you knew where it was. But I have known the well's location for days. I even discovered a backway in through the forest. A faster way. And I was here before you all," he bragged.

"If you knew where the well was, why have the natives continued to dig?" I asked.

He laughed. "I may have learned the location of the well, but I couldn't yet put my plan into motion. For that, I had to be patient. I had to await your arrival."

"It was you, wasn't it?" Hadrian charged. "You who poisoned us? Why? To get back at me for not telling you about the location of the well?"

"You didn't poison everyone to get us to come here," Logan said.

"Perhaps not entirely, but you know why I did that," Alrik countered.

Confusion crossed Hadrian's face. "If you didn't taint the water for revenge, then why did you do it?"

Logan answered his question. "Payton's flash drive was stolen while she lay sick."

Hadrian was still confused. "Her flash drive? What is that? Is it something to do with her hands?"

It was obvious now that he hadn't been the one to take it. "Hadrian, I'm sorry," I said. "I'm sorry I even remotely suspected you of taking it."

"Why would I take it? I don't even know what it is."

"In our world," Logan explained, "a flash drive is a small device you plug into a computer. It stores information on it. Documents, pictures, stuff like that. Payton wore one around her neck. She's had it since we left our world. She was never without it."

"I wrote stories on my computer and saved them on it," I told him. "In one of the worlds we were in, I was able to write about our adventures in another realm. For days, I didn't realize we weren't even in our world. Not until we saw the three moons."

Hadrian shook his head as understanding dawned on him. He glared at Alrik. "You poisoned everyone to get to Payton? To get that flash drive thing?"

"I saw in your tent that you had a laptop," I said to Alrik. "I hardly thought it would still be working, but I guess I was wrong?" I was fishing for answers. If he'd seen what was on that drive, he'd know about the gifts from the well. I had to hope that even if his device worked, it wouldn't be compatible with my world's technology. Although he'd read my journal. That much was obvious. And it mentioned the gifts too.

"I know everything about the powers granted by the wishing well. At least what you put down. First, I had to search through ridiculous stories until I got to your escapades."

That dashed my hopes. I was too concerned about what he read to be insulted.

"What powers? The well grants wishes?" Hadrian said.

"And now I know!" Alrik continued. "Hadrian

has the gift of direction. He can go anywhere. Home, other worlds, back and forth through time, and still return here."

"What are you talking about?" Hadrian demanded.

"Don't play dumb with me," Alrik hissed. From the folds of his cloak, he suddenly produced a gun and aimed it at each of us. "Now is the time for answers. I've waited long enough."

"This is between you and me. Leave them out of it," Hadrian snapped.

"No, it's between us all," Alrik insisted. He aimed the gun at Hadrian. "You are going to take me home." Then he swiveled the gun between Logan and me. "And you two will come along and show me how to complete the ceremony for the gifts."

"There is no ceremony," I said, eyes fastened on the weapon. Logan was tense beside me and I knew he watched the gun as well, waiting for an opportunity to strike. "And to be honest, I don't think the gifts will work in your world."

"Why not?" he demanded, lips curled in a snarl.

"You told me your world has no moon," I reminded him.

"Never mind the fact that even if it did, it could take years for the timing to work. Twice in a blue moon is rare," Logan said.

"Decades even," I added.

Alrik pointed the gun at Hadrian again. "I can go anywhere with him along. We will go world to world until we find the twice blue moon."

"The moon isn't actually blue," I said. The concept would be hard for him to understand since he'd never experienced moon phases. He may have read about the secrets of the well, but he didn't quite understand how it all worked. No doubt, this explained his need for Logan and me to accompany him. I supposed I should be grateful for that, at least. Otherwise, he'd have no use for us.

Alrik appeared to ponder that for a moment, and then a look of dawning crossed his face. "Oh, I know. The world where you make wishes. Take me there. I will wish to find a twice blue moon, and then we will complete the ritual. Once I have my gift, I won't need any of you. I will... let you all go," he said.

Yeah, right.

"That's not going to happen," Hadrian said. "None of us are going anywhere with you."

Alrik emitted a low growl sound in frustration. "Show me how to make the wish," he said to me, pointing the gun at Logan again. "Or I will kill him. I know how much he means to you."

"You kill him, and I have no reason to show you anything," I vowed.

"Or, I can always hurt him, and in order to save him, *your precious love*, you will do my bidding," Alrik determined.

My face flamed red, I was sure. But he was right. I would do anything to save Logan. If he killed him, he would kill any chance he had at making me cooperate. But if he wounded him, then I would be forced to help him in order to save Logan.

"You're a real twisted son of a — " Logan snarled.

Hadrian leaped forward suddenly, reaching out toward Alrik.

Alrik moved back but stumbled. A shot rang out, making me scream and Hadrian cry out in pain. The three of us went down — Logan positioning his body in front of me protectively. In tune to my emotions, my hands roared to life, one a flaming torch, the other icy cold.

"Look at what you did!" Alrik screamed. "How is any of this supposed to work without Hadrian to take me where I need to go!"

From my position, I could see Hadrian, blood pooling around him as he tried to stem the flow from his leg with his hand. We had to do something. Now.

"You will pay for this. With your life. I don't need you anyway." Alrik had the gun pointed at Logan now.

Though I was mostly hidden from Alrik's view,

I could see through the bent up crook of Logan's arm that Alrik meant what he said with deadly intent. I wasn't about to let that happen. He was unprepared when I gave a grim nod to Logan, and he ducked down in time for me to aim a fireball at our assailant.

"Bullseye!" Logan hollered when the flames exploded against Alrik's chest and lit him up. Engulfed by flames, he screamed. He stumbled, arms flailing, then seeing no other discourse, he ran and dove head first into the well and was gone.

"Good riddance," Logan said. He rushed to peer over into the watery depth while I took stock of Hadrian's injury.

It was bad.

CHAPTER 20

The bullet had hit Hadrian in the leg, and blood continued to pool around him. From the amount that scorched the ground, I knew it'd hit a main artery, and time wasn't on his side.

Logan came over and knelt beside me. He whipped off his shirt and tied it tight around Hadrian's leg like a tourniquet. Thankfully, it slowed the rush of blood.

"I...I think I'm done for," he said, his face a sheen of sweat but pale as the moon.

"Don't say that," I begged, my guilt overwhelming me.

"Tell me," he said. "What he meant. About the gifts. The wishes."

I guess it didn't matter now if he knew. If Alrik had been right, and Hadrian did possess the gift of direction, it was possible he may not even know. If he did have the gift, however, knowingly or not, then it may explain his ability to find his way home and back. And that thought, fleeting as it was, made the ache in my gut a little more wrenching. It may mean what Alrik had said was true — we'd never find home without Hadrian.

"It's complicated, and there's a bunch of things that have to align in order for it to work," I began. Logan and I exchanged glances, and I knew he was thinking the same as me about my healing gift in the medieval world.

"You can only make a wish 'twice in a blue moon' if that makes any sense to you," Logan said.

Hadrian gave a grim nod. Whether it meant he understood, I couldn't tell.

"You also have to get some of the well water on you," I said. "Do you recall at any time that you or someone else made a wish about always finding your way home or anything like that?"

"No," he said. "I don't remember anyone ever making wishes on a well."

"In my world, a wish was made when I was young, about remembering. And I carry this gift of recollection with me always. Like a photographic memory for written words, and also for words spoken aloud. But, in each world I enter where a counterpart of me exists, I assume their gift as well, at least for the time I'm in that world."

Hadrian stared at me, mesmerized. "Incredible."

"It's why I didn't know for a while what I could do here—with my hands. I had to figure it out," I continued.

Hadrian turned his gaze on Logan. "Do you have gifts too? Oh, yes, you said you could fight."

Logan smiled tightly. "No. My gift isn't from the well. I trained in my world. Practiced, studied. Channeled my anger into skill."

"The gifts aren't always so great," I said. "They can be unpredictable and have devastating consequences." Like Sir Gregor.

Hadrian nodded in understanding.

"When I went searching for you guys, I brought my journal—the one you lent me to write in. It contained handwritten notes about the last worlds Logan and I were in. I didn't know that Alrik had stolen it until I became sick with the poisoned water." I rushed on, not wanting to think about how I'd suspected Hadrian for Alrik's misdeeds. "In the journal, I mentioned the well and the wishes and the gifts. And I talked about the flash drive." I paused a moment. "This is all my fault. Alrik did all this because of me."

"No," Hadrian put his hand on mine. "You weren't the only one with secrets." His breaths became pants, and perspiration dripped from his chin. He raised his hand off mine and gestured around. "This...

world was of our making. Everything."

"What?" Logan and I said.

"I knew where the well was because this is my world. Well, not precisely. But the future of my world. It was practically a blank slate when we arrived — my family and I. Almost everything here has been brought through from other worlds. We tried to rebuild it — our home. The people, the animals. Everything."

"You brought everything here?" I repeated his words. "I don't understand."

"I lied to you both. The well isn't a dead end." His gaze implored us to forgive him. "Through the well, we brought eggs, plants, seeds. Borrowed — no — stolen from other places. When we first came through, we ended up here, and it took us a while to realize this was our world's future...not its past as we'd first thought. The trees and brush were overgrown. Nature had taken back the land, but those ruins... we knew what they were. They were part of the structure where we once lived — my family."

"But you said your world had all those moons," I argued.

"Yes, and one had exploded, causing so much chaos, but that had been so long ago. Then, all but one of them exploded, and it destroyed everything. Or, at least, we thought it had. We escaped into the well when we saw what was happening. My mother and father and my brother and me. We took refuge in these caves. The hieroglyph was carved by my father, for future generations to remember how to go back and forth. My people — we all knew that we could travel from world to world. And when my world met its end, most of us had fled. Though, many chose to stay behind, thinking our technology would save them. They were wrong. We figured that out because afterward, we went back to search for survivors. Again and again, we returned. But nothing. No one. We'd hoped others would find their way here eventually, but no one came. And then my family became sick. One by one, they died, leaving me alone. So I made a new family.

"The natives," Logan said. "They were from other worlds like this one."

"Yes. I'm ashamed to say I brought them here. Tricking, coaxing, or bribing them to come with me so I wouldn't be alone. I chose them for their innocence. The way they loved the land and were part of it. I guess I feared if others did come, others like those from my world, then the same things would happen again. Not total destruction, but advancement. The way we lived…it was wrong. We cared more for our comforts than our world. We were greedy, destructive."

"I get where you're coming from," I told him. "Trust me, we can relate."

"My parents wanted a new world. A better

world. Where people and nature could coexist."

"Your family brought those birds here?" Logan asked, making a face.

Hadrian laughed, making his complexion turn paler. "Eggs, we brought eggs. We didn't expect them to multiply like that."

"Hadrian, how old are you?" I asked. There were clansmen and women older than him, at least in appearance. But if what he said was true, then it meant he'd been here for a lot longer than any of us had realized.

"We age slowly in my world. If you age like the people I've brought here, then every ten years or so of your life would equal one year of mine."

"Wow, that would make you about two hundred years old in our world," Logan told him.

Enough time to cultivate a world, I guessed.

"My original world is the only one I know of that this age anomaly occurred."

"I don't know how I would feel about living for so long," I admitted. And now I realized why Hadrian had been so desperate for us to remain. So many years, he was alone except for the clan, who he was determined to keep the same for fear of the advancement that had corrupted his world the first time.

"Why all the weapons?" Logan asked suddenly.

We'd passed several rooms of weapons which I

assumed had been 'borrowed' from other worlds.

"Even before Alrik arrived, we knew others may come — others that weren't like-minded as us. And that could mean dangers. We had to keep this world safe. Do you understand?"

The look on his face made my heart pound in fear for him. "Of course," I assured him.

He stared into my eyes. "You can get home."

"Pardon?" I asked.

He looked down at the ground. "I'm sorry. I've known all along about the tethers, and I should have told you. You both have been right to be suspicious of me. I haven't told you the truth. I would have, I promise. I just wanted a bit more time." Logan reached for the canteen that had fallen to the ground in the scuffle. He uncapped it and helped Hadrian to drink. Hadrian nodded his thanks. "The tethers are real — in a way. What you can't see from the drawings is the people holding or wearing tokens from our world."

"Tokens? What do you mean?" Logan asked.

I feared I'd been correct when I assumed there'd been something from our world we should have brought with us to get us back.

"Like a key?" I supplied. "We didn't bring anything like that with us." I knew my tone was desperate, which made me feel worse, considering poor Hadrian was dying before our eyes.

"No. Not a key. Anything. Like a pebble or a feather, even a book or pen, something from the world you left. It's how I always return here or navigate to other worlds that I want to revisit. I simply take something along with me. Then when I enter the well, I'm faced with only one choice of doors. Our world knew that secret, at least."

"I'm confused," I admitted. "What exactly happens when you dive into the well? Like, where did Alrik go?"

"It depends," Hadrian said. "He may be facing many doorways. But if he had your flash drive on him, he very well may have gone to your world."

"What!" Logan and I gasped.

"When you enter the well, you must swim down, following a short underwater canal. Then, you come up into an underground cavern, like depicted on the hieroglyph. From there, if you carry a token, then only one door will present itself. Otherwise, there will be several."

"That's messed up," Logan said.

"It can be," Hadrian admitted. "For the most part, I never knew where I was headed when I left to get supplies, and sometimes it could take a while to find the well so that I could return. Though, when you come and go through the well, as opposed to the tunnels that you guys arrived from originally, the well is usually located close by."

"That's handy," I said. Recalling how I'd had to search for it a couple of times.

"Yes. And, like I said, if there's a world that I intentionally wanted to go to, I simply brought with me a token from that place."

"Leaving you to face only one doorway," Logan said.

"Yes." Hadrian's voice was getting weaker.

"All this time, we had the way home right in our grasp," I said. "And now it's gone."

"We didn't know," Logan said, trying to make me feel better.

"I'm dying," Hadrian said. "This world will go on. And now that Alrik's gone, it will be safe without me here to protect it."

"What can we do for you," I said, a sob catching in my voice.

Logan and I each took one of Hadrian's hands in ours.

"Go home, be happy," he told us.

"But we can't," I said. "We've nothing else from our world to see us home." Alrik had the last laugh, after all. If he'd survived.

The sounds of shouts reached our ears. Torchlight lit the area off in the distance.

"They're coming," Logan said grimly. "Alrik's

tribe." He got up and grabbed the gun Alrik had let fall to the ground. Checking the chamber for bullets, he shook his head at us. "Empty."

"You must go," Hadrian said.

"Where? When they discover Alrik's gone and find you here…" Logan didn't want to finish his sentence.

"I'll be dead," Hadrian said.

"They'll come after us. We can't return to the camp. We'll put everyone in danger again," I said.

"We'll have to take our chances in the well," Logan said grimly.

"You… can go home," Hadrian insisted.

"No, Alrik stole our chance," Logan said.

"You have something from your world to take you back," Hadrian gasped. "Something else you've had all along. You have each other."

"What do you mean?" I asked.

"Hold tight to each other," Hadrian said. "See yourselves home."

And with those last words, he lay back and breathed no more.

He was gone.

But he'd granted us a gift in his final moment. The way home.

As the natives broke onto the scene, shouting and rushing around frantically in their search for their leader, Logan dropped the gun and reached out his hand to me, pulling me to my feet.

And together, we jumped into the well.

CHAPTER 21

Logan and I swam, deep and swift, as though our lives depended on it. Then, just as I feared I would run out of air, we surfaced in a cavern, just as Hadrian had described. There were no signs of Alrik along the way, not in the water or in the cavern. We pulled ourselves ashore and rested, chests heaving, gulping air. So great was my exhaustion. I wanted only to lie still and sleep, even if just for a moment or so. But seconds later, Logan was tugging on my arm. I cracked an eye and peered at him.

"Look!" He pointed at the cavern wall where a single door sat nestled in the stone.

We exchanged glances, not knowing if we should dare to hope.

"Ready?" he asked, pulling me to my feet.

I nodded, and we crept forward. He reached out and turned the handle, and together, hands still clasped, we walked through.

We stepped into a short tunnel, at the end of which was another single doorway.

Cautiously, we approached, and as I studied the exit, it didn't appear to be a door at all, but something else. When I thought I'd cry out from the suspense of it all, Logan lifted his hand and touched what appeared to be something blocking the exit.

"It's… the barn door," he croaked.

Not taking his word, I reached out as well and touched the rough wood, which I now realized leaned precariously against the exit. Could it be? I dared to hope. Allowing just a glimmer of sweet expectation to seep into my weary bones.

"This is a good sign," Logan said as we maneuvered the barn door that obscured our view just enough to squeeze around. I helped him to move it back into position.

Now, darkness surrounded us. We had no light to guide our way. Since Logan again held my left hand, I willed my right one to heat. But nothing happened.

"No fire power," I informed him.

"We'll have to make our way in the dark, then," he said.

"Okay," I agreed. "But instead of heading toward your basement, let's go to the station house." If that was indeed what waited at the end of the tunnel. If so, then we could scope out the house from the outside and look for any anomalies.

Fumbling our way ahead by reaching out and trailing our fingers along the packed dirt walls, we soon came to the end of the line.

"Stairs, going up," Logan informed me, though I'd noticed them as well.

The way was narrow and steep and when Logan went first, I didn't object. He let go of my hand and held onto the railing, which I did as well. At the top, he slowly opened the creaky door.

We came up into the train station, the smell of musty warm air greeting us as we entered within. It was dim, but faint light crept through the window, guiding our careful steps.

"The station house," he said as I moved beside him. "I think this is it." His voice was filled with wonder. "I think we're home."

Home.

Could there be any more comforting, kinder word than that?

Logan shivered, and we smiled at each other.

"We'll have to find you a shirt," I said over the lump in my throat.

As we moved toward the exit, part of me was afraid to hope. We'd done this dance before, come into a world we'd thought was ours, only to be wrong. What if we faced that world again? Or another just like it, similar to ours, and yet, not quite?

I froze suddenly. "Logan, we should have taken something from Hadrian's world. A stone or something, so we could return. Maybe bring help?" If we returned, we'd have to go through the well, but I was sure since this appeared to be our world, then we'd find the well near that Fed cabin, just out of town.

He sighed and gave my hand a squeeze. "We both know it's too late for him. Besides," he fumbled in his pocket and pulled out a pebble, "I thought to grab this."

I felt a tear slip down my cheek as I smiled up at him.

With his last words, Hadrian had saved us — it appeared. We owed him so much.

We paused before leaving the station house and again exchanged a glance.

"The moment of truth," he said, opening the door. We both stepped out into the muggy air. The ground appeared wet, as though it'd recently rained. Overhead, gray and black storm clouds swirled and gathered, threatening to pour.

We moved around the building and stared across the back lawn toward the house. A couple of lights were on upstairs and down.

"Looks like someone's home," I said, my voice quiet.

"I...I don't know what to do," Logan admitted. "What if my mom's there?"

"Then we'll know we're not home." But another idea struck me. "Hey, if your mom is there, then maybe we're in the genie world. If your wishes start again, you can wish us home."

He nodded and smiled a bit. "There is that." Then, he sighed and looked up. "It's probably too early in the day to see how many moons there are. It's too cloudy anyway. It's about to let loose overhead. Let's go." I noticed he shivered again.

Halfway across the yard we were in luck as a pair of shirts and some shorts Logan's size were pegged on the clothesline. They were damp but not soaking, and Logan pulled a shirt over his head. The clothes we had on were probably wetter, considering our recent swim.

As we got to the back door, Logan reached for the door handle and paused.

"Get ready to run," he warned. "Just in case." He slowly cracked open the door and eased through first. I followed. We were in the kitchen, and we weren't alone.

"Finally!" a voice exploded. "Where were you? We looked and looked. Megan! Callie!" It was Kevin.

Logan and I just stood there frozen.

"Hey, why'd you change?" Kevin asked. "Are you guys wet?" He came over to inspect us. "And is your hair longer?"

Logan ran a hand over his head self-consciously. "I... dunno. Maybe."

Megan burst into the kitchen. "Oh, you guys! That was epic!"

Callie came next and winked at me. "Totally. Where'd you guys hide? We searched every inch of the place."

"We..." I began as Dan and Jake entered the room next.

"You guys!" Jake laughed, shaking his head.

"We'll never tell," Logan interrupted, giving me a look.

Our friends circled around us, noticing our state. Kevin reached out and touched a strand of my hair.

"Yep, it is longer," he stated.

"Okay, come on, spill," Callie insisted.

Logan laughed a little. "Okay, we give. And yeah, our hair is wet, and that's why it looks longer. We went through the tunnel to the station house."

"No way. Impossible. Dan and Kevin searched there," Megan informed him.

"We cheated," I admitted. "We went over to the cemetery."

"You were supposed to stay inside," Karena said as she strode into the kitchen, joining us. "And..."

gross!" She hated the cemetery.

All of us laughed. It felt so good to be surrounded by our friends again.

And then, in that moment, it dawned on me. Logan and I stared at each other while we both realized nothing had changed. We had returned to almost the exact time we'd left, even though months had passed for us.

Yet, that had happened in the genie world, too.

By the shadow that suddenly crossed Logan's face, I think he had the same thought.

"Hey," he said, snagging one of the dying flowers in a vase on the table. "Karena, make a wish."

She stared at him strangely but shrugged. "Okay, I wish I had a million bucks." After she blew on the flower, sending petals flying, she held her hand out expectantly and closed her eyes tight, only to open them a second later and stare at her palm.

Logan's glance turned to me, and I tensed.

When I didn't do the genie thing, we both smiled.

"So much for that," Karena said. "Who's turn to hide?"

"I think I've had enough of hide and seek," I said, silently vowing to never play again.

"Yeah, and it's getting near dinner time. We better go," Kevin said to her.

"We'd better head out too," Megan said to me.

I didn't want this moment to end.

"Hey, are you okay?" Dan asked. "You shouldn't have made her go out to the cemetery, Logan."

"Yeah, especially in the rain," Megan agreed. "You look tired."

"I'm fine," I said. "Really. Just been a long day. I'm glad to be back. Group hug, okay?"

Laughing, we all pulled in close and hugged.

"We'd better head out too," Callie said, looking pointedly at Dan and Jake.

"I wish my dad was back," Logan said, "he could drive you guys to the lake."

"It shouldn't be cold out," Kevin said. "Or is it?"

"Ah, no, it's not bad," I said. "It looks about to rain again, though."

"Great, I thought it stopped," Callie said, running a hand over her hair.

We all headed toward the living room, grabbed up our cells from the table, and went to the front door where all our shoes were. I resisted the urge to go through my phone like everyone else was doing. I noticed Logan had left his on the table.

Everyone started getting ready to go, and I stared at Logan, not ready to leave him yet.

"Um, Payton, you were gonna stay for dinner tonight, remember?" Logan said, casting me a lifeline.

"Oh, yeah. I totally forgot," I said.

"Probably all the excitement from the cemetery," Jake said with a laugh.

"I guess," I agreed.

Soon, everyone piled outside and began heading down the driveway. Logan and I watched them from the open door, the moment surreal.

Megan turned back suddenly. "Hey, I thought you guys were in the basement. There was some thumping going on down there."

"Wasn't me," echoed the others with shrugs.

"Anyway, Payton, we'll talk later," she said pointedly.

"Yeah, I'll call you."

A moment later, Logan shut the door and locked it.

I went over to the table and put my phone with his. Then we went back into the kitchen, where Logan grabbed a long knife from a wooden block. Next, he grabbed a sturdy rolling pin from one of the drawers and passed it to me.

We moved to stand at the basement door.

Without words, we both knew what threat we could be facing.

We'd made it back, but there was another who also could have come through.

Alrik.

CHAPTER 22

Logan eased open the basement door, and sure enough, we heard noises below.

"Maybe we should call the cops and let them deal with him," I suggested quietly, suddenly regretting my decision to ditch my phone.

"No way. Too risky. What if it is Alrik, and he starts blabbing about the tunnels. He could easily show the cops exactly what he means." I suppose I failed to look convinced since he continued. "Not to mention the fact he could tell them you set him on fire."

"Do you really think he'd squeal about the tunnels?" I didn't even want to consider the condition of him since the fireball fiasco. Anyway, I refused to own any guilt over that. Our lives had been at stake, and Hadrian had paid the ultimate price for Alrik's demand for answers.

"Who knows what he's capable of. And even if he doesn't, I have no doubt he's mad enough to try and have you put away."

He was probably right. "So, how do you suppose we deal with him?"

"He's not armed, at least not with a gun. But who knows what else he had going on in that cloak of his. You stay up here, okay? I can handle him on my own," Logan said.

"I have no doubt, but we're both exhausted after walking for days with hardly any sleep and not much food. Plus, he could have a hammer or something. Your dad's got a lot of tools down there."

"Damn it, my dad. He could be home any second."

Logan, not wanting to wait any longer, motioned for me to stay put while he began descending the stairs. The light had been left on, and after I saw him reach the bottom, I crept down a couple of steps and sat, the rolling pin tight in my grip. The way the staircase was built against the basement wall on one side allowed me to look through the bars of the railing to the other side and see the large main room. Other smaller rooms branched off it.

It didn't take long before I heard Logan's voice and a gasp of surprise. "Hey! Stay where you are unless you want a world of pain."

Seconds later, I heard Alrik's unmistakable voice. "How did you get here? Did you follow me?"

He sounded confused and confrontational but not in considerable pain, so I assumed the well water had doused the flames before they did much damage.

I couldn't help it. I had to creep further down the stairs until I could see what was happening. They faced each other, about five feet separating them, both wearing scowls on their faces.

"I came with a message for you from Hadrian," Logan said. Then, still holding the knife in his hand, he moved forward, spun around lightning fast, and kicked Alrik right in the face.

He went down like a ton of bricks.

Logan stood over him, legs spread wide, in a ready stance I'd seen him use during tournaments. Feeling safe to descend the remaining steps, I approached the pair.

"Logan," I said, letting him know I advanced. He'd always warned me not to come upon him too quickly when he was in fight mode, just in case I was mistaken for an enemy.

He turned his head slightly and, seeing me, gave a nod. "He's out cold."

I came up beside him and stared down at Alrik with distaste. From where I stood, I could see blood at the corner of his mouth. Other than that, he didn't appear to be hurt. His clothing was damaged—his cloak scorched, and the white shirt beneath blackened with soot.

Logan's breaths came out like angry sighs, and I touched his arm with my free hand.

"It's okay. I know you're mad. I am, too. But I have to be honest, despite how much we cared for Hadrian and how much we'll owe him for the rest of our lives, I have to wonder." I took a deep breath, too, debating if I should say out loud what I suspected.

Logan looked at me. "What?"

"I have to wonder if Hadrian would have told us the way to get home despite what he said...if he hadn't been dying."

A bunch of emotions seemed to play across Logan's face, denial, frustration, regret, and then resignation. He stared back at Alrik, and his features hardened again.

"You know I'm right. Even though it sounds terrible to say it now," I said.

Refraining from voicing his thoughts, he gave a brief nod instead.

"It doesn't mean that we owe *him* anything," I verified, gesturing at Alrik.

"I would like to think that Hadrian would have told us on his own."

Giving his arm a squeeze, I said, "I'm sure he would have. One day. That was some incredible story he told us about his world and what he and his family did to create a new one."

"It was," Logan agreed. "What do you think we should do with him?" he meant Alrik.

I shrugged. "Drag him back into the tunnels?"

Logan appeared to ponder the idea. "Hey, you know what? I think that's actually a good idea. Let some other world deal with him."

Logan held out his hand for the rolling pin. He put it and his knife on a workbench. Then he bent down by Alrik, maneuvering him to get hold of his upper body, and raised him in his arms. "Take his feet," he said.

I stepped around them, keeping a close eye on Alrik's features in case he woke.

We moved through the doorway leading to the tunnel, and Logan jostled momentarily as he snagged a flashlight and put it under his arm. He walked backwards, and the glow was aimed ahead of us so we could make our way in semi-light. It didn't take long to reach the old barn door. We set Alrik down, and we both slid the door over enough to allow all of us to pass through.

When we started down the tunnel, a tremor of foreboding washed over me.

"Do you think this is a good idea?" I ventured.

Logan's head moved up and down in the affirmative. "We'll toss him through the first door we find."

"And then what? Hope to hell he doesn't just open it up and come back through?"

After a few twists and turns, we saw a doorway. Stopping before it, we set Alrik down and stared at each other.

"I don't think it's enough to toss him in," I said. "There's no guarantee the rooms will rotate in time to keep him away."

Logan frowned. "You're probably right. Hadrian said something about keeping it under an hour, and I think he'll be awake before then. If he was even telling the truth about that," he added in afterthought.

"Let's take him in and see how far from the door we can get him. Maybe if he's far enough from it, it'll give the worlds enough time to rotate before he goes through?" I suggested.

After a moment of thought, Logan agreed. "Okay, ready?"

I nodded once, and he reached for the door.

It appeared to be night, wherever it was, so Logan shone the flashlight over the landscape. Overhead, the sky appeared clear and dotted with stars. The ground, from what we could make out from the doorway, looked normal enough. Hilly with trees and shrubs, it could easily be mistaken for Trent.

Logan shoved the light under his arm again

and maneuvered Alrik into his grasp. I picked up his booted feet, which made a sloshing noise, and we moved through the doorway.

Over my shoulder, I kept looking back, hoping and praying we weren't making a mistake.

CHAPTER 23

Keeping in a straight line, we walked for what felt like an hour, but was most likely ten minutes or so. I'd lost sight of the doorway a while ago.

"At least we should still arrive in our world right when we left," Logan said. His breaths weren't coming out strained like mine.

"That might only be when we return through the well," I said, my teeth gritted. My bones ached, I was so tired, and my sight was getting blurry.

Logan stopped suddenly, and I felt Alrik's body jerk a bit, whether, from the motion of us carrying him or his own power, I wasn't sure.

Then Alrik groaned.

Quickly, we set him down.

I moved away from his prone form, but Logan shone the light on him and started going through his pockets and searching through his cloak.

"What are you doing?" I hissed, wanting to get

away as fast as possible.

"Looking for the flash drive," he hissed back. "If he jumps in the well, it's a sure way back."

He was right. I knelt and started searching as well.

"Success!" Logan said, waving my lanyard with the drive attached. I snatched it and stuffed it away.

"Okay, great, let's go," I said.

"Wahhht," Alrik groaned, reaching out with his hands.

Logan stood up. "Payton, turn around."

"Why?" I asked suspiciously.

"Just do it," he implored.

Seeing the determined look on his face, I turned away.

Next, I heard a snap and a scream.

Then Logan was grabbing for my hand and we started running, Alrik's curses following in our wake.

We didn't slow until we saw the open doorway. By that time, I had to switch to a jog. It may have been a trick of the light, but it looked like the door was slowly closing.

"Hurry!" Logan urged.

With a last burst of strength, we bolted ahead and dove through the door just as it slammed shut behind us.

I braced my hands on my knees, gulping in air.

Logan still held the flashlight, and it appeared we were in the tunnel we'd recently left, but it was hard to tell.

"We have to hurry if everything's changing," Logan said.

He grabbed hold of my hand again, and we retraced our steps, rushing as fast as we could.

Finally, before us, we could see the open doorway partially skewed by the old barn door.

"It's moving," I cried. Seeing less and less of the opening appearing visible.

Logan was practically dragging me by this time. With one last leap, we flung ourselves through just as the barn door slid back into place.

I couldn't talk. Only take in deep breaths of air while I bent forward, arms wrapped around my belly.

"Are… are you okay?" Logan gasped.

At least he sounded winded.

I couldn't speak, so I nodded.

Then, with slow, measured steps, we moved down the tunnel and went into his basement.

"That was close," Logan said.

"Too close."

"Logan?" we heard a call from above.

Logan stared at me, and I saw him swallow hard, no doubt over the lump in his throat.

"Dad? We're down here," he finally answered.

"Payton with you?" his dad called down.

"Yeah," Logan called back.

"I brought dinner home," he said. "Pizza, okay?"

Logan looked at me, and though I felt a tear slip down my cheek, I smiled and nodded.

"Pizza's great," Logan said.

Together, hands clasped, we headed upstairs.

Julie is a long-time resident of Hamilton, Ontario, where she lives with her husband of 25 years. She has two grown sons who recently left the nest. Working in a library for several years inspired her to pursue her long-time love of writing. Please check out her website julieparker.net

www.ingramcontent.com/pod-product-compliance
Lightning Source LLC
Chambersburg PA
CBHW051829170626
46807CB00003B/1097